**…do anything for you. You know that,
…?" Emilio said.**

…hed out and brushed his fingers gently against
…eks. Pleasure shot straight to her core, tickled and
…her.

…you want me to carry you back to my estate?"

…s not and say we did," she said with a laugh. "In case
…haven't noticed, I'm a curvy woman, not a toothpick,
…I don't want you to hurt yourself."

…tare was bold, penetrating. Emilio didn't speak,
…t utter a word, but if looks could kill she'd be six feet
…er. Sharleen gulped. *What did I do wrong? Why is he*
…

…tense moment only lasted a few seconds, but it felt
…hours had passed.

…io broke the silence, his voice hollow, cold as ice.
…didn't raise his voice, but his disappointment was
…ent. "You're an incredibly smart woman, but I swear,
…etimes you say the craziest things."

…leen narrowed her eyes and hitched a hand to her
…"Who are you calling crazy?"

…. Now shut up and kiss me." Emilio seized her
…t, wrapped his arms around h…………her lips
with his mout…

Dear Reader,

After I lost my second child, I attended group therapy sessions, and seven years later I still remember a single dad with a heartbreaking story of loss. I thought about him as I wrote *Seduced by Mr. Right* and knew the book was going to be a sweet, tender romance about two wounded souls who help each other heal. I enjoyed seeing the transformation in Emilio Morretti once he met Sharleen Nichols, and I cheered them on as their relationship progressed. It's touching to see them open up to each other, and once they bare their souls, things REALLY heat up. I have a feeling you're going to love chapter sixteen, too! ☺

Special thanks to everyone who purchased The Morretti Millionaires series. I am humbled by your messages, reviews and words of encouragement. Look for more Morretti Millionaires books in the near future.

I love to hear from readers, so drop me a line at pamelayaye@aol.com, find me on Facebook or visit my new, revamped website at pamelayaye.com.

All the best in life and love,

Pamela Yaye

Seduced
BY MR. RIGHT

Pamela Yaye

H HARLEQUIN® KIMANI™ ROMANCE

Recycling programs
for this product may
not exist in your area.

ISBN-13: 978-0-373-86393-8

Seduced by Mr. Right

For questions and comments about the quality of this book please contact us
at CustomerService@Harlequin.com.

H HARLEQUIN®

Printed in U.S.A.

™ www.Harlequin.com

Pamela Yaye has a bachelor's degree in Christian education. Her love for African-American fiction prompted her to pursue a career in writing romance. When she's not working on her latest novel, this busy wife, mother and teacher is watching basketball, cooking or planning her next vacation. Pamela lives in Alberta, Canada, with her gorgeous husband and adorable but mischievous son and daughter.

Books by Pamela Yaye

Harlequin Kimani Romance

Visit the Author Profile page at Harlequin.com for more titles.

Acknowledgments

Shannon Criss: Thank you for giving me the freedom to write the story that was in my heart. I appreciate your support and hope you'll be my editor for many years to come. We make a fantastic team! ☺

Daniel Odidison: You are the best dad ever!!! Thank you for being my unofficial PR person. You tell everyone you meet about my books and hand out autographed copies at the bank, the grocery store, church and in mall parking lots. You are just amazing, and I'm SO thankful you're my dad.

Chapter 1

"Emilio, we have a problem."

Frowning, Emilio Morretti hit Pause on the remote control and glanced over his right shoulder. Sunshine splashed through the windows of his Greensboro estate, filling the living room with a harsh, blinding light. But he could still make out his business manager's silhouette in the open doorway. Emilio was drained, but he nodded his head in greeting. Today was the second anniversary of his nephew's death, and although his spirits were low, he slapped a smile on his face.

"Hey, man, what's up?"

"Sorry for barging in like this, but this couldn't wait." Antwan Tate slipped off his aviator sunglasses and rested his leather briefcase at his feet. Antwan reeked of confidence. His black Tom Ford suit didn't have a wrinkle in sight, and he was wearing more bling

than Diddy. The men had known each other for years—
ever since Emilio relocated from Italy to Atlanta in
2006—and he could tell by his manager's creased brow
and stiff posture that he was stressed-out. Over the
years, they'd become closer than brothers, and Emilio
considered Antwan family. Antwan had been there
for him during his darkest days, and he trusted him
wholeheartedly.

"What's going on?"

"You need to look at this," Antwan said, offering
him a large manila envelope.

Emilio stared at it but didn't touch it. "What is it?"

"It's a letter from the Internal Revenue Service. It
arrived at my office this morning by courier, and once
I spoke to the other parties involved I drove straight
here."

Reluctantly, Emilio took the envelope from Antwan's
outstretched hand and opened it. As he scanned the
letter, his heart began beating harder, faster. Unable
to believe what he was reading, he looked at his manager closely, searched his face for signs of decep-
tion. A known prankster, Antwan took great delight
in punking his friends, but this time Emilio wasn't
falling for it.

Determined to beat Antwan at his own game, Emilio
crumpled the paper, tossed it over his shoulder and
hit Play on the remote control. Cheers, laughter and
shrieks of joy filled the room. Emilio never got tired of
replaying his nephew's soccer games, and he grinned
every time Lucca's image filled the eighty-inch TV
screen. Two years had passed, but Emilio still couldn't
believe that Lucca—his adorable nephew with the curly
hair and high-pitched giggle—was gone.

Emilio leaned forward, gazing intently at the TV. The DVD was cutting in and out from being played so much, but his nephew's celebration dance at the end of the game was his favorite part of the video. He chuckled at Lucca's antics. Emilio wondered what he'd be like today if he were alive. He would have been in the second grade, and no doubt faster on the soccer field.

"Throwing away the letter isn't going to make the problem go away…"

Emilio tuned his manager out, pretended he wasn't there. Pain stabbed his heart like a knife. His throat closed up, becoming dry and sore. Emilio stared at the TV with a heavy feeling in his chest, wondering for the umpteenth time how he could have been so irresponsible that afternoon, so damned reckless. *I screwed up, and it cost me everything I hold dear,* he thought. *I'd do anything to have Lucca here. Anything at all.*

Hanging his head, he raked a hand through his short, thick hair. He tried to channel positive thoughts, but nothing came to mind. Every morning, he woke up thinking the accident had been a horrible dream, but the moment he realized his nephew was really gone, he broke down. *Why did Lucca have to die?* He looked up at the ceiling as if the answers to his questions were written there. *I miss him so much it hurts.*

"We need to come up with a plan," Antwan continued. "Before it's too late."

Emilio lowered his head and kept his gaze on the marble floor. He didn't want Antwan to know his emotions had gotten the best of him—again. When he least expected it, grief overwhelmed him, and there was nothing he could do about it. He was a broken man, consumed with regret, and his pain was constant, always there. Pulling himself together, he straightened his shoulders and cleared his throat. "Nice try, but I'm too old to fall for your stupid pranks."

"This isn't a prank." Antwan picked up the wad of paper, dropped down in the chocolate-brown armchair and flattened the letter on the glass coffee table. "This letter from the IRS is real, and so is this 2.5-million-dollar tax bill."

"That's impossible," he said, convinced his manager was trying to pull the wool over his eyes. "Monroe Accounting has been doing my taxes since I moved to Atlanta, and every year they assure me that everything is kosher."

"Well, it isn't." Antwan undid the buttons on his suit jacket and leaned forward anxiously, as if he were waiting for Emilio to bring *him* up to speed.

"I had an hour-long conversation with the IRS. Monroe Accounting claimed tax shelters that the IRS disallowed, and because of the error you owe the IRS 2.5 million dollars."

"How can I be punished for their mistake?" Emilio fumed, struggling to control his temper. It wasn't about the money. He'd trusted his accounting firm, and now they'd screwed him over—big-time.

What else is new? said his inner voice. *People have been screwing you over ever since you won your first championship race. You should be used to it by now!*

"I didn't do my taxes," he pointed out. "Monroe Accounting did."

"I know, it sucks, and I'm all for suing their asses, but first we have to get the tax man off your back." Antwan loosened the knot on his royal blue tie. "I've had clients in trouble with the IRS before, but nothing like this. This is bad, Emilio, *real* bad."

No, it's not. Bad is giving the eulogy at a five-year-old's funeral.

"If you disregard the letter, the IRS could seize your bank accounts, freeze your assets and sell them at auction. I've seen it happen, and it isn't pretty…"

Fear pulsed through Emilio's veins. *I can't lose my estate. It's filled with great memories of Lucca and I sense his presence here.* He thought of all the times they'd played air hockey in the media room, the nights they'd camped out in the backyard, the Spider-Man-themed birthday party years earlier. He had raised the child as his own and cherished the times they'd spent together. Losing his estate was unthinkable.

"Pay the bill, and fire those idiots at Monroe Accounting ASAP."

"We can't. It isn't feasible right now."

"Why not?"

"Because the bulk of your fortune is tied up in real estate and long-term investments, and if you liquidate your stocks, you'll lose hundreds of thousands of dollars."

It took a moment for Antwan's words to sink in. They hadn't talked about his finances in months, not since the last time they'd argued about Emilio's spending.

"Am I broke?"

"No, but if you pay the IRS you'll only have a million dollars left in your bank account."

"I can live off of that money for years."

Antwan scoffed. "Not if you continue supporting

Francesca and your other relatives. You'll be lucky if that money lasts three months."

His manager was right. His kid sister was always asking him for money, begging and pleading for short-term loans she never paid back. But Emilio didn't mind. He enjoyed spoiling her, figured it was the least he could do after what had happened to Lucca. His family meant the world to him, and he wasn't going to stop helping them because his stingy business manager had a problem with it. "Like I said, that's plenty. If I need more funds, I'll let you know."

"Or you can come out of retirement and make more money. You could compete in the World Series Racing All-Star Race in August. A win would catapult you back to the top, where you belong."

"It's not going to happen, so save your breath."

"Why not?" he pressed, his eyebrows raised. "If you get back in racing shape you can compete for another five or six years. That's a ton of cash *and* championships."

Emilio didn't respond. Staring out the window, he watched birds soar across the clear blue sky. He hadn't been outside in weeks—not since his run-in with that crazed photographer on his estate. He considered going for a jog once Antwan finally left. But when his manager started talking business, there was just no stopping him, and Emilio feared he'd badger him about coming out of retirement for the rest of the day.

"Don't you want to see if you still got it? If you still have what it takes to compete at the highest level, with the best competitors in the world?"

"No. I'm content here, and I don't want to return to the track." It was a lie, one he'd been repeating for the

past two years. But he couldn't tell Antwan the truth—
not without feeling ashamed. So he shut his mouth and
dodged his manager's gaze.

"I'm worried about you."

"Don't be. I can take care of myself."

"Don't you think you've punished yourself long
enough?" Antwan gave him a stern look. "It's time
to quit moping around the house and rejoin the land
of the living."

Emilio strangled a groan. This wasn't the first time
Antwan had talked to him about his future, and it probably wouldn't be the last. Deep down, he missed working on his beloved race car, traveling the globe with his
pit crew and meeting the die-hard World Series Racing fans who followed him from one city to the next.
But his devotion to the sport had cost him Lucca, and
he'd never forgive himself for what had happened to
his nephew. *I don't deserve to be happy. Not after causing the death of such a fantastic kid.*

"I have a surefire plan to rejuvenate your career,"
Antwan insisted. "And it starts with the All-Star race.
To get the ball rolling, I've arranged a meeting with
Ferrari next month, and they're pretty stoked about
seeing you again."

Curiosity got the best of him. "They are?"

"Of course they are! You're one of the greatest World
Series Racing drivers of all time, and your old sponsors
are desperate to have you back."

Emilio balked, told himself he didn't care. He couldn't
do it, wouldn't do it, and there was nothing his manager
could say to change his mind. He was sick of his family
and friends giving him unsolicited advice, and he wished
everyone would leave him the hell alone. Annoyed, he

considered asking Antwan to leave, but he wisely bit his tongue. His manager had been in his corner for almost a decade, and without his steadfast support Emilio wouldn't be a three-time champion, or one of the most recognized athletes in the world.

"Have you given any thought to the TV interview with Italia Sports?" Antwan asked. "If I don't give them an answer by four o'clock today the deal is off the table."

"Tell them no dice."

"But they doubled their offer."

"Am I supposed to be impressed?"

"Man, do it," Antwan implored. "That's a hundred grand for an hour of your time, and they're willing to interview you here at the house. That's a sweet deal."

Emilio stood his ground. "Tell Italia Sports I said thanks, but no thanks."

"Are you attending the Exotic Car Show in Miami on Memorial Day weekend, or is that out of the question, too?"

"Maybe next year."

Antwan nodded, said he understood, but he looked sadder than a kid who'd lost his lunch money on the playground. A terse, awkward silence ensued. To break the tension, Emilio clapped his friend on the shoulder and said, "Let me get you a drink." He stood, dropped the remote control on the couch and strode purposely across the living room. After entering the bar, Emilio opened the fridge, grabbed two beers and unscrewed the tab from one.

"You hung up more pictures of Lucca," Antwan said, glancing around the room.

"Yeah, I found them on my old BlackBerry device and printed them off."

"You've made this place your own personal shrine to him."

Ignoring the dig, Emilio admired the picture prominently displayed on the fireplace mantel. It had been taken the day of Lucca's preschool graduation, and every time his gaze landed on the photograph he felt an overwhelming sense of pride…and guilt. His nephew had been on cloud nine that day, and even after all these years he could still hear Lucca's laughter as they ran around the jungle gym playing tag.

"Are you going to the cemetery this afternoon with Francesca to release balloons?"

Emilio nodded. "Yes, I'm going to pick her up at two o'clock—"

The telephone rang, and a long-distance number flashed on the TV screen. It was his cousin Rafael calling from Washington, DC, and although they hadn't spoken in months, Emilio didn't answer the phone. Francesca loved family gossip and had told him just yesterday about the birth of Rafael's first child—a baby girl named Violet—with his wife, Paris St. Clair-Morretti. The news still boggled his mind. His cousins Demetri, Nicco and Rafael had found true love and were completely devoted to their partners. And according to Francesca, Nicco and his wife, Jariah, were expecting, and Demetri was planning the wedding of the century with his fiancée, Angela Kelly. *I hope my invitation gets lost in the mail, because there's no way in hell I'm going to Demetri's over-the-top wedding.*

"The guys are meeting at Halftime Bar on Friday night to celebrate Jamieson's promotion." Antwan sat down on a stool, grabbed one of the beers and took a swig. "You promised you'd be there, so don't even *think* about flaking on us."

Antwan's concerns were valid. Emilio often broke plans at the last minute, and it had earned him a reputation for being a mood killer. Going out in public made him nervous, and on the rare occasions that he met up with his golf buddies, he always regretted it. Gold diggers flocked to him in droves, and the more he spurned their advances, the more aggressive they were. "I'll come, but I can't stay long."

"Why? Got a hot date with Ginger?"

"Man, please, she's ten years my junior. And she's my sister's best friend."

"I know," Antwan said with a sly wink. "But you like curvy women, and that girl has booty for days!"

Yeah, and a thirst for wealth and stardom that could rival a reality TV star! Emilio wasn't interested in the British nanny, and every time she dropped by his estate unannounced, he ordered his butler to send her away. Francesca was determined to hook them up, but Emilio was even more determined to keep his distance. Ginger was nipping at his heels for one reason and one reason only: to get her hands on his fortune. But Emilio wasn't having it. He hadn't been intimate with anyone since his nephew's death, and he'd rather watch home videos of Lucca than hook up with his sister's pushy roommate. "I'll be there."

"You better, or I'll drive back out here and kick your ass."

"I thought you were a lover, not a fighter?" Emilio joked.

"You know it!" Antwan popped his shirt collar. "I couldn't have said it better myself!"

Chuckling, the men bumped fists and bottles. Emilio couldn't remember the last time he'd laughed, and it felt good to crack a joke with Antwan. His reprieve didn't last long, though. His mind wandered, filled up again with thoughts and images of Lucca, and his good mood fizzled. *What am I doing? I shouldn't be yukking it up. My nephew died, and it's my fault.*

The doorbell rang, and Antwan jumped to his feet as if his bar stool were on fire.

"I'll get it," he said, leveling a hand over his suit jacket.

Emilio put down his beer. "Who is it?"

"Your new life coach."

"My new *what*?"

"You need someone to help you get your life back on track, and Sharleen Nichols is the perfect person for the job."

To thwart his escape, Emilio stepped in front of Antwan. He folded his arms across his chest and stared him down. "Are you out of your mind?" he asked. "What were you thinking inviting some strange woman to my estate?"

"Sharleen isn't a stranger. I've known her for years. She's worked with several of my other celebrity clients, and they all sing her praises."

Emilio wasn't impressed, not one bit. He sensed Antwan was romantically interested in this life-coach friend. That surprised him, because in all the years they'd known each other, he'd never seen Antwan excited about anyone. Not even the models he routinely hooked up with.

"Sharleen graduated from Duke University with honors," he boasted, checking himself out in the mirrored wall behind the bar. "She's one of the most passionate, energetic people I've ever met, and gorgeous, too. You're going to get along great. I can feel it."

"Don't count on it," Emilio mumbled.

Chapter 2

Peace and tranquillity showered over Sharleen Nichols as she drove through the private gates of the lakefront estate on the edge of Greensboro, Georgia. A light breeze whistled through the magnolia trees dotting the manicured grounds, and sunflowers perfumed the morning air. The stone-and-brick mansion was nothing short of perfection, and the property screamed of opulence and wealth. *This isn't a house; it's a compound,* Sharleen thought, driving up the long, winding driveway. *No wonder Emilio Morretti rarely goes out. This place is a dream. If I lived here I'd never leave!*

Sharleen parked behind Antwan's SUV and turned off the engine. Last night she'd reviewed her notes about Emilio Morretti—the troubled race-car driver with the jaw-dropping good looks—and although she was prepared for their consultation, butterflies danced in the pit of her stomach. *I can't blow this. My boss is depending on me. And if I want to be considered for the vice-president position, I have to prove that I'm a go-getter, a closer.*

To calm her nerves, Sharleen closed her eyes and breathed deeply through her nose. News articles and magazine covers scrolled through her mind. Emilio Morretti was a third-generation race-car driver, and one of the most electrifying World Series Racing competitors of all time. Championships and fame had come fast and furious, and during his fifteen-year career he'd shattered one world record after another. According to the press, he was a quick-tempered man with expensive tastes who fancied models as much as exotic sports cars. At thirty-five, he was one of the most eligible bachelors in the country and also a bona fide star in his native Italy. Or at least he used to be. Two years ago, he'd walked away from the sport that brought him fame, fortune and international prestige, and he'd turned his back on his fans.

Sharleen grabbed her leather Birkin bag and got out of the car. She knew better than to believe everything she read online, especially on celebrity gossip sites. But there was no disputing the facts. Emilio Morretti was on a self-destructive path, and if he didn't change his ways, things would only get worse. In recent months, he'd had several run-ins with the paparazzi and had allegedly slugged a photographer for trespassing on his property. True or not, the gossip painted him in a bad light, and Antwan was deeply worried about his superstar client. He'd told her that Emilio was still struggling to cope with the loss of his nephew, and since

Sharleen specialized in grief and trauma, she'd agreed to work with him.

That wasn't the only reason, her conscience pointed out. *Mrs. Fontaine didn't give you much of a choice, and if you blow this assignment you could lose your job!*

Last month, during her annual performance review, her boss had implored her to drum up more business, or else. Sharleen tried not to dwell on her problems—it wouldn't be fair to Emilio. And besides, things were looking up. She was speaking at a women's business luncheon tomorrow and manning the Pathways Center booth at the Mind, Body & Soul Conference on Saturday, so that would definitely bring in more clients.

Perspiration dotted her forehead, and her legs were shaking, but she strode confidently up the walkway, as if she were on top of the world. She'd learned a long time ago not to wear her heart on her sleeve.

Sharleen pushed her eyeglasses up the bridge of her nose and straightened her black power suit. Ignoring her erratic heartbeat, she climbed the steps and rang the doorbell. When no one answered, she began to fear that Antwan had forgotten about their ten o'clock meeting. She took her cell phone out of her purse and accessed her contacts list.

The door swung open, and Antwan stood in the grand foyer, dressed in one of his trademark suits, grinning from ear to ear. "Good morning, beautiful."

Sharleen held up her cell phone. "I was just about to call you. I thought maybe you forgot about our appointment."

"I could never forget you. You're my future baby-mama, remember?"

"Yeah, right! Life coaching is my first and only love, so you're fresh out of luck, my friend."

"Just wait. One day you'll be singing another tune!" *No, I won't. Men and careers just don't mix.*

"I'm glad you're here." Antwan gave her a hug, one that lasted longer than necessary, and kissed her cheek. "Have any trouble finding the place?"

"No, as usual your directions were bang on. Thanks, Antwan."

"Don't sweat it. You know I got you."

After taking her hand, he led her inside the mansion. Everything in the vestibule gleamed and sparkled. The foyer was dripping in gold, and it was elegantly decorated with Italian furnishings. Crystal chandeliers hung from the ceiling, and the vintage lamps, decorative bowls and glass sculptures were eye-catching. The air smelled of hazelnut coffee, and the heady aroma made Sharleen think of her parents.

Memories of her childhood played in her mind. She thought of all the mornings she'd made breakfast with her mom, the summer days she'd helped her dad wash his rusted, old Buick and their family movie nights at the local drive-in. Biting the inside of her cheek kept her tears at bay, but there was nothing she could do to alleviate the crushing pain in her heart.

"After we finish up here, I'm taking you out for lunch," Antwan announced. "I was at Sushi Huku a few weeks ago, but it just wasn't the same without you."

"I can't. I have another consultation at noon."

He made a puppy-dog face, but Sharleen wasn't moved. Antwan was used to having his way with women, but his childish antics had never worked on her. Not even when she was a lonely college graduate with no friends and a broken heart.

"Tell me something." Eyes narrowed, he studied her like a painting hanging in the Metropolitan Museum of Art. "How come you shoot me down every time I ask you out?"

Oh, brother, not this *again.* Sharleen groaned inwardly, but maintained her bright, everything's-great smile. Dating Antwan had never crossed her mind. Not once. Why would it? He collected women like trophies, and she wasn't interested in being his flavor of the week. "Knock it off," she quipped, playfully swatting his shoulder. "I came here to meet Emilio, not shoot the breeze with you."

His grin was back. "I rarely get to see you, so I figured I'd kill two birds with one stone."

Dodging his gaze, she turned toward the pale blue walls to admire the framed photographs hanging above the mahogany side table. There were pictures of family barbecues and birthday parties, and even a Christmas-day wedding. The images were touching, not at all what she'd expect to see inside Emilio Morretti's estate. Again, Sharleen thought of her parents. *They always loved the holidays, especially Christmas—*

"This cat-and-mouse game has gone on long enough." Antwan leaned in close and affectionately squeezed her forearm. "Why are you playing hard to get?"

Who's playing? Sharleen respected Antwan and valued their friendship, but they could never be more than friends. He didn't have a faithful bone in his body, and if he ever discovered her secret, he'd run for the hills.

Didn't they all? She was damaged goods to the opposite sex, and that would never change. Although Sharleen longed to have a family of her own, she knew she had a better chance of winning the lottery than finding her one true love. No matter. Advancing her career was all that mattered, all she cared about. Being a life coach was her passion, and she woke up every morning excited to go to work. She wished she had more time to spend with her girlfriends, but she wouldn't change her life for anything in the world.

"Where's Emilio? We have a lot of ground to cover this morning, and I'm anxious to get started." To prove she meant business, Sharleen took a clipboard and a pen out of her purse. "Are you going to take me to Emilio, or do I have to find him myself?"

Antwan wagged a finger in her face. "We'll talk later, because this isn't over."

Oh, yes, it is. You and I would never work, so quit while you're ahead!

Sharleen spun on her heels and was surprised to see that Emilio Morretti had silently entered the vestibule. Her heart stopped dead in her chest. Her head felt fuzzy, as if she was hungover, and her pulse beat out of control.

To look that fine should be criminal, illegal in all fifty states.

He had creamy olive skin, thick eyebrows and the most beautiful eyes Sharleen had ever seen. They were soulful, a light brown shade, and tinged with gray around the edges. Dark stubble covered his jaw, and although he was casually dressed in a white polo shirt, loose-fitting pants and leather sandals, there was no disputing his dashing looks.

Good God. I didn't think it was possible, but he's even more attractive in person than he is on TV! He had chiseled features, a head full of dark hair and a body that would make Hercules jealous. Antwan was the one in the designer threads, but Emilio was the one who reeked of power and affluence. He had a guarded vibe, and he didn't look happy to see her. But for some inexplicable reason Sharleen was drawn to him anyway.

Her skin tingled with desire. Sharleen wanted to introduce herself to Emilio, but the words didn't come. Her thoughts were racing, her breathing was labored and her tongue wouldn't move. She ordered herself to quit gawking at him, but she didn't have the strength to turn away.

"This beautiful young woman is your new life coach. Isn't she stunning?"

Her cheeks burning with embarrassment, Sharleen glared at Antwan. She hated when he made a fuss over her, but instead of whacking him upside the head with her purse, she stepped forward and extended a hand to Emilio. "Thank you for inviting me to your lovely home. I'm thrilled to be here." Sharleen heard her voice crack, but she continued. "Antwan's told me a lot about you—but don't worry. I never believe a word he says!"

A grin dimpled Emilio's cheek, yet he didn't laugh. She could tell he wanted to—his eyes were smiling, and his nose was twitching—but something was holding him back. He took her hand in his and held it for all of five seconds. Yet it was long enough to make her body quiver. Sharleen didn't make it a habit to drool over her celebrity clients, but everything about Emilio Morretti turned her on. His full lips, his broad, strapping shoulders, his quiet disposition.

"The pleasure is all mine, Ms. Nichols."

Her breath caught in her throat. *Ooh, that voice!* His Italian accent was a sensuous treat, and the sound made her heart flutter in her chest like a butterfly. Her gaze strayed to his mouth, lingered there for a beat. Every inch of her body was aroused, infected with lust, and her legs felt rubbery, as if they were about to give way. She was nearly undressing him with her eyes, couldn't stop herself from admiring his fit physique. *Knock it off—he's a client!*

"Welcome to my estate."

Her nipples hardened, strained against the soft, silky material of her satin bra. She wondered how it would feel if Emilio kissed her, imagined his hands stroking her body. Sharleen slammed the brakes on the illicit thought. *What's the matter with you? Why are you acting like a desperate housewife?* In the five years she'd worked at Pathways Center, she'd never been attracted to a client or ever crossed the line. Her desire for Emilio scared her, made her question if she could work effectively with him. *Thank God our weekly sessions are on the phone and not in person,* she thought, sighing in relief. *Because with those eyes, and that voice, there's no way I'd ever be able to concentrate!*

"I feel terrible that you drove all this way, but I won't be needing your services."

His words turned to garble in her ear. *Is this a test? Am I being punked?*

"Emilio, she just got here. Give her a chance." Antwan sounded like a teacher exasperated with a troublesome student. "I wouldn't hire Sharleen if I didn't think she could do the job."

"I don't need a life coach." He didn't raise his voice, didn't lash out, but there was no mistaking his anger.

His forehead was creased, and his mouth was a firm, hard line. "I can run my own life, and I don't need you, or anyone else, telling me what to do."

Emilio aimed his gaze in her direction, but he seemed to look through her, not at her. He made her feel unimportant, and Sharleen didn't like it one bit. *But what am I supposed to do? Throw a hissy fit and demand he talk to me, not at me?*

"It's not my job to tell you what to do." Her voice quavered with emotion, but Sharleen was determined to speak her mind. "My goal is to help you overcome your grief and rediscover your purpose in life. I'll support you and hold you accountable, but I won't boss you around or cram my opinion down your throat. I'm a life coach, Mr. Morretti, not a bully."

Surprise showed on Emilio's face. He gave her the once-over but didn't speak. His eyes were weapons of mass destruction, dark and dreamy, but Sharleen didn't wither under his piercing stare. Her heart thumped so loud her ears throbbed, and it was hard to think when he was looking at her like *that. This is what I get for watching HBO last night,* Sharleen thought, chastising herself. *That erotic movie excited me, and now I can't think of anything* but *kissing Emilio!*

Sharleen cleared her mind and deleted every conflicting thought. She couldn't afford to screw this up; her boss was counting on her. During her performance review, Mrs. Fontaine had given her an earful, and every day her searing rebuke played in Sharleen's mind.

"As a senior life coach it's your responsibility to help build the business, develop new strategies and create buzz on social media, and sadly you're not carrying your weight..."

Three weeks after her review, Sharleen was still pissed. *What does Mrs. Fontaine expect me to do? Hold celebrities at gunpoint and make them sign up for a free consultation?*

"Let's sit down and talk," Antwan proposed, gesturing to the living room.

Emilio shook his head. "I can't. It's time for my morning workout."

"All I need is fifteen minutes of your time." Sharleen held up her clipboard and flashed her brightest smile. "Once you finish answering this brief questionnaire, I'll be on my way."

"I'm not interested." Emilio gave her his back and addressed Antwan. "I'm going into my gym. Let yourself out, and please show Ms. Nichols to her car."

Before Sharleen could say "It was nice meeting you," Emilio Morretti was gone. Antwan strode into the living room, returned seconds later with his briefcase and hustled her back through the foyer. Without a word, he opened the front door, ushered her outside and closed it behind him.

"I'm sorry about that." Antwan smiled apologetically. "Don't take it personally. Today's the second anniversary of his nephew's death, and he's angry at the world right now."

Sharleen nodded. "That explains a lot."

"You've worked wonders with some of my other high-profile clients, and I'm hoping you can do the same with Emilio," he said, his eyes alight with interest. "There's tons of money to be made at the World Series Racing, and time's running out for Emilio's big comeback."

"He has to be ready and willing to change. I can't force him."

"You can't treat Emilio like your other clients. He's a special case."

You can say that *again! He's tall, dark and handsome, and he sounds delicious, too!*

"I know you normally do your sessions by phone, but I need you to be more hands-on with Emilio, more accessible." Antwan took his sunglasses out of his back pocket and slipped them on. "Weekly phone calls and emails aren't going to cut it either. It's a bitch getting him on the phone, and these days he rarely uses his computer."

"What do you expect me to do? Club him in the head with my Birkin bag and drag him down to my office?"

Antwan chuckled. "You're as saucy and feisty as ever!"

"I'm serious. I'm a life coach. Not a fairy godmother. There's only so much I can do."

"You're one of the most persuasive people I've ever met, and if you can't convince Emilio to come out of retirement, no one can."

"That's not why I'm here. I'm here to help him fulfill his dreams."

"All he's ever wanted was to be a race-car driver. Losing his nephew shook him to the core, but I'm confident he can be a champion again." Antwan continued his pitch full speed ahead. "Do your weekly sessions here at his estate and treat Emilio like a friend, not a client."

His know-it-all tone irked her. "I can't drive to Greensboro three days a week. I have other clients and obligations to fulfill—"

"What if I sweeten the deal?" He cocked his head

and flashed a devilish grin. "If you convince Emilio to come out of retirement, I'll give you a $10,000 bonus."

Sharleen felt her eyes widen in surprise and her mouth fall open.

"Emilio and I are meeting at Halftime Bar on Friday night, and I want you to join us. Hanging out with him at his favorite pub will definitely help break the ice."

"Antwan, I can't," she said, finding her voice. "I already have plans."

He cocked an eyebrow. "With whom?"

"We're having a retirement party for my uncle, and if I'm a no-show, my aunt Phyllis will beat me like I stole something!"

"Great sacrifices produce great rewards. Isn't that your personal motto?"

Sharleen hit Antwan with a pointed look. He was twisting her words, but she didn't have the time nor the patience to debate the issue with him. Her priority was her family, and she wasn't going to let Antwan make her feel guilty for having a personal life. "Maybe next time."

"Fine, suit yourself." His tone carried a bitter edge, but he smiled and waved as he hopped into his SUV. "I'll be in touch. Take care."

Sharleen unlocked her car door and slid inside. Deep down, she wasn't upset that Emilio had kicked her out of his estate; she was relieved. *It just wasn't meant to be,* she decided, shrugging her shoulders. But all wasn't lost. She had two more consultations lined up for that afternoon and several booked for later that week. Unlike Emilio, those clients were eager for professional help and desperate to change their lives. Encouraged, Sharleen turned on the engine, cranked up the radio and exited the tree-lined estate.

Chapter 3

Pathways Center was in an attractive plaza filled with glitzy boutiques, cafés and beauty salons. It had several high-end stores, and as Sharleen left Samson's Gym on Friday morning, she noticed the parking lot was packed. It was only ten o'clock, but the plaza was filled with couples, well-dressed businessmen and children begging their parents for toys and ice cream.

It was another warm spring day, and Sharleen felt invigorated by the signs of the season. The air held the scent of flowers; the sky was free of clouds and gleaming with sunshine. Strolling down the street, soaking up the sun, Sharleen greeted everyone she passed with a nod and a smile. Exercising always improved her mood, and even though she wasn't as flexible as the other women in her Stiletto Aerobics class, doing high-kicks in her favorite pair of Jimmy Choo shoes made her feel invincible, as if she could conquer the world. *And I will,* she vowed, fervently nodding her head. *I'm going to get that VP position if it's the last thing I do!*

Reaching Pathways Center, Sharleen pushed open the door and strode inside. Attractive furniture, European artwork and vibrant area rugs decorated the waiting area. Waving to the receptionist, Sharleen collected her messages and continued down the hallway, anxious to get down to work.

Entering her office, she dropped her tote bag on the couch and opened the window blinds. Sunshine spilled into the room, making the space feel warm and bright. Her gaze landed on the red sports car double-parked in front of the bank. Emilio Morretti's face popped into her mind, and try as she might, she couldn't get rid of the sexy image. She'd thought of him last night and wondered how he was doing. Had he given any thought to what she'd said, or was he still in a miserable funk? Sharleen considered calling Antwan to find out but struck the idea from her mind. She had a busy day ahead of her, and she didn't have time to shoot the breeze with her friend.

At her desk, she turned on her computer and took out her leather-bound journal. For the rest of the morning, Sharleen reviewed client profiles, updated her schedule and edited her online newsletter. Hours slipped by, and when lunch came and went she decided to take a break. Eager to speak to her colleague and best friend, Jocelyn Calhoun, she scooped up her desk phone and punched in her number. She'd left Jocelyn two messages yesterday, but still hadn't heard back from her. That was unlike the social-media queen. Her iPhone never left her side, and she always responded to texts within seconds—unless she was watching *Dating in the City.*

"Hey, girl, it's me," Sharleen said, tapping her pen absently on her desk calendar. "I haven't heard from you all day and just wanted to touch base. Give me a ring, or swing by my office when you get in. I'll be here for the rest of the day, so stop by. We *really* need to talk."

Hanging up the phone, she glanced at the wall clock above the door. Her next session didn't start for an hour, but if she was going to survive her conversation with the disgruntled housewife from Malibu, she needed to meditate. Like exercising, it was an unshakable part of her daily routine, and she felt ineffective without it. Sharleen loved her career and couldn't imagine ever doing anything else, but being a life coach was emotionally and mentally draining.

Unbuttoning her blazer, she kicked off her sandals and sat back in her chair. Blocking out the noises around her, she closed her eyes and exhaled every stress, every anxiety. Sharleen turned toward the window and welcomed the sunlight as it warmed her face. As her thoughts cleared and a sense of peace washed over her, she reflected on the events of the past week. *There were plenty of lows, but only one high.* Desire flared inside her body. *Forty-eight hours after my disastrous consultation with Emilio Morretti, and I'm still thinking about him. That's insane! He's curt and serious and...and...oh, so dreamy. I wish he was my man.*

For the second time in minutes her thoughts went off track. In her mind's eye, she saw Emilio stalking toward her. His gaze was intense, and he was wearing a broad grin. One so captivating it made her skin tingle and her heart soar. Emilio took her in his arms, held her close to his chest and caressed her cheeks with his fingertips. Licking her lips, she waited anxiously to feel the pleasure of his kiss. He lowered his mouth to hers, and—

"Ms. Nichols, are you okay?"

Her eyes flew open. Embarrassed that her boss had caught her daydreaming, Sharleen stuffed her feet back into her shoes and stood. "Good afternoon, Mrs. Fontaine."

"May I have a word with you?"

Adjusting her glasses, she fervently nodded her head. "Yes, of course."

"This won't take long." Her boss, a petite woman with mocha-brown skin, had a no-nonsense demeanor and impeccable style. As she marched into the office, her wavy hair and leopard-print scarf flapped around her. Her colleagues gossiped that Mrs. Fontaine and her second husband, Jules, were having serious marital problems, but Sharleen didn't believe them. Her boss looked chic and well put together, not like a woman having man trouble.

"Please have a seat." Coming out from behind her desk, she gestured to the glass table beside the window. "Would you like something to drink?"

"No, thank you. I'm fine."

Mrs. Fontaine sat down on one of the wrought-iron chairs, and Sharleen did the same.

"Over the years, you've become good friends with Ms. Calhoun, and I want to ensure her departure doesn't cause you any unnecessary grief."

Confused, Sharleen furrowed her brow. "Her departure? I'm afraid I don't understand."

"I'm surprised she didn't tell you."

"You're surprised she didn't tell me what?" she repeated, wishing her boss would quit talking in circles and tell her what the hell was going on. Sharleen knew Jocelyn was worried about her mother's health and wondered what had happened.

"Has she taken a leave of absence?"

"No. Ms. Calhoun has been relieved of her duties."

Sharleen struggled to find her voice. "B-b-but everyone loves her," she stammered. "She's the best life coach here and—"

Mrs. Fontaine scoffed. "No, she's not."

Oh, that's right. Brad is. He's your favorite. He's everyone's favorite. Sharleen despised Brad McClendon, and that would never change. When he wasn't talking trash about her to their colleagues, he was stabbing her in the back and trying to steal her clients. All because she'd spurned his sexual advances at last year's Christmas party. His boy-next-door charms fooled everyone— including their boss—but Sharleen saw through his phony, I-love-everybody facade. He was a know-it-all, with an ugly attitude, and she didn't trust him.

"I didn't come here to gossip. I came to discuss your career." Mrs. Fontaine clasped her hands around her knees. "You're a valuable member of the Pathways team, and I have high hopes for you."

You do? Really? Then why are you so hard on me?

"I hope you're not still upset about your performance review last month…"

Sharleen was, but she would never admit it. She didn't want Mrs. Fontaine to think she was overly sensitive, so she dismissed her boss's concerns with a flick of her hand. "Of course not. I appreciate your honesty, Mrs. Fontaine, and your thorough assessment of my performance. I love working here, and I'm going to do everything in my power to promote this wonderful, life-changing center."

Mrs. Fontaine's face came alive and visibly relaxed. "That is wonderful news. You looked upset after our meeting, and I feared you were going to quit."

"You can't get rid of me *that* easily," she joked. "I'm one tough cookie!"

Mrs. Fontaine laughed, and Sharleen did, too. Her joke lightened the mood, and the tension in the air abated. They spoke about ways to attract new clients and how to boost staff morale. Moments of levity with her boss were few and far between, and she enjoyed their one-on-one time. Finally, after working together for years they were starting to make some headway.

"I look forward to working with you and the rest of the Pathways team for many more years to come." As Sharleen spoke, her boss's smile got bigger, brighter. Encouraged, she went on. "I'll miss working with Jocelyn, but her departure won't have a negative effect on me. I'm committed to my clients, and I'd never do anything to impede their personal growth."

"As you know, I'm expanding our services and planning to open centers in Seattle, Houston and LA later this year," she said proudly. "I'm going to need someone I can trust to be my vice president, and I wanted you to know you're one of the top contenders for the job."

Sharleen wanted to break out in song, but she squelched

her excitement. "When will you make a decision about the position?"

"By the end of May, if not sooner."

Great! That gives me eight weeks to prove I'm the perfect woman for the job.

"I better go." Mrs. Fontaine glanced at her gold wristwatch and rose from her chair. "I need to speak to Brad about Emilio Morretti before he leaves for the day."

Oh. Hell. To. The. No! Sharleen surged to her feet. She didn't want to get on Mrs. Fontaine's bad side, but she had to set her boss straight. "I met with Mr. Morretti on Wednesday morning, and he made it very clear that he doesn't want a life coach."

"He's still grieving the loss of his nephew. He doesn't know what he wants." Her tone was brisk, matter-of-fact. "Mr. Tate has given us a lot of business over the years, and *we* can't afford to disappoint him."

Sharleen wanted to roll her eyes, but she nodded her head in understanding. *One minute we're sharing a laugh, the next she's taking jabs at me. Go figure!* Mrs. Fontaine's words were a veiled insult, a slap in the face, but Sharleen didn't argue. She saw the bigger picture, understood what was at stake, and knew if she played her cards right there'd be a promotion in her future. Listening with half an ear, she considered her next move.

"Mr. Tate is a successful business manager, and every time one of his celebrity clients is photographed leaving our center the phones ring off the hook!" Dollar signs twinkled in her eyes. "Brad is a stellar life coach. He can get through to Emilio Morretti. I know it."

And what am I? Chopped liver? Her body tensed,

and her mouth curled in disgust. Pressing her lips together to trap a curse inside, she fumed. *If I lose another client to Brad I'm going to scream!* On the surface
Sharleen remained calm, but she was annoyed with her
boss and angry at herself. If she'd signed Emilio on
Wednesday, instead of making googly eyes at him,
she wouldn't have to go toe-to-toe with Brad for *her*
client. "I deserve to be Mr. Morretti's life coach. I spe-
cialize in grief and trauma, and furthermore, I booked
the initial consultation."

"But he dismissed you shortly after you arrived at
his estate."

Sharleen winced, as if in physical pain. *What the
hell? Is Antwan my friend or not?* She didn't appreciate him talking to Mrs. Fontaine behind her back and
planned to tell him just that the next time she saw him.

An idea came to her in a flash. Bingo! That was it!
She'd have drinks with Antwan and Emilio at the Halftime Bar and convince Emilio to sign with her. *It's either that, or lose him to Brad-the-blue-eyed-schemer!*
Sharleen felt guilty about missing her uncle's retirement party, but she couldn't give Brad the upper hand,
not with the VP position at stake.

"I'm meeting Mr. Tate and Mr. Morretti tonight to
finish our consultation." The lie came out of her mouth
in a breathless, nervous gush, but she continued full
speed ahead, before her boss could question her. "I'm
confident Mr. Morretti will sign with us once I tell him
more about our top-notch, award-winning agency."

Her boss gave her a bewildered look and scratched
her head. "I'm confused…"

Sharleen gulped. Her palms were slick with sweat,
but she maintained her poise. She desperately needed

another crack at Emilio Morretti. But when she opened her mouth to plead her case, Mrs. Fontaine raised a hand to silence her.

"I spoke to Mr. Tate at length this morning, and he never mentioned your meeting."

"He's a very busy man. It must have slipped his mind," she said, shrugging her shoulders good-naturedly. The fib fell off her lips with ease, sounding plausible, convincing, too. "Since Halftime Bar is only a few blocks from here, I'm planning to head straight over once I finish my last session of the day."

Her boss's nose wrinkled in distaste. "You're going to meet Emilio Morretti dressed like that?"

"Is there something wrong with my outfit?"

"Not if you're going to a funeral!" she scoffed, her thin lips curved in disapproval. "Emilio Morretti is an international superstar and one of the sexiest bachelors in the world."

"And?" Sharleen asked, puzzled. "What does his relationship status have to do with me?"

"I want you to knock his socks off, and that boring, navy blue suit isn't going to cut it…"

You're a fine one to talk! You always wear pantsuits!

"Your outfit does nothing to enhance your curves."

Sharleen touched a hand to her fitted, three-button blazer. "But this is Chanel!"

"I don't care," Mrs. Fontaine snapped, sounding exasperated. "Put on some makeup, get rid of that hideous hair bun, and for goodness' sake, show some cleavage!"

Sharleen cracked up. She couldn't help it. Mrs. Fontaine was in her thirties and was a chic dresser with a unique sense of style, but the more her boss encouraged her to "sexify" her look, the harder she laughed.

"You have a great figure, but you dress like some-one twice your age," Mrs. Fontaine complained. She paused, as if deep in thought, then adamantly shook her head. "I take that back. My mother's sixty-one, and she dresses *way* sexier than you."

Oh, my goodness, she's serious; I thought she was joking!

"I'll give you one more crack at Mr. Morretti, but if he blows you off again, Brad's in, and you're out. Understood?"

Sharleen nodded and stepped aside to let Mrs. Fontaine pass. She was happy to see her boss go. Her next session was about to start, and now she had a business dinner with Emilio Morretti to prepare for, too. Mrs. Fontaine marched down the hall without another word and disappeared into the staff room.

Slumping against the door, Sharleen released a deep sigh. This was her last chance to impress Emilio Morretti, but she wasn't going to dress like a Pussycat Doll to get his attention. She was better than that. And besides, she didn't own any tight, low-cut dresses.

I'm not sexy, that's why. I could never pull off that kind of look.

Sharleen dismissed the outrageous advice Mrs. Fontaine had given her seconds earlier. More determined than ever to prove her worth—and land that coveted VP position—Sharleen stalked over to her desk, snatched up her phone and punched in Antwan's number.

Chapter 4

Where is everyone? Emilio glanced at his platinum wristwatch and scanned the waiting area for his golf buddies. He had a gnawing feeling that something was amiss and sent another text message to Antwan. His friends were thirty minutes late, and if his seafood appetizer hadn't tasted so damned good, he would have left a long time ago.

Signed jerseys hung from the ceilings, country music blared from the overhead speakers and a tantalizing aroma consumed the air at the sports bar. Emilio was sitting at a corner booth, far away from the other patrons, but he felt them staring at him, watching him on the sly. A redhead sashayed past his table, switching her hips and flipping her hair, but he ignored her. He didn't want female companionship. He enjoyed sitting alone at the back of the lounge—thinking about Sharleen Nichols.

For the first time in years, he didn't ponder his nephew's death or his overwhelming sense of loss. Instead, images of the bubbly life coach with the infectious smile filled his mind. The Southern beauty had an aura of youth and vitality, and if he hadn't been in a miserable funk on Wednesday he would've spent the rest of the morning getting to know her better.

Emilio tasted his soda. Though his conversation with Sharleen had been brief, she'd made an indelible impression on him. She was full of personality—a bundle of excitement and positive energy that intrigued him. She was *just* that lively, that appealing and engaging. He didn't date and hadn't been intimate with anyone since losing his nephew, so his attraction to Sharleen shocked him.

Emilio considered what he'd learned about Sharleen in the past forty-eight hours after an extensive online search. The Duke graduate was everything Antwan had said, and more. She was active in the community, passionate about health and wellness and a self-described foodie. Her Instagram page was filled with recipes, pictures of her gourmet kitchen and her closest friends. He liked that she wasn't obsessed with money and fashion like the women he'd hooked up with in the past, and he wondered if she was dating anyone.

Why do you care? You kicked her out of your estate, remember?

Emilio felt like an ass for the way he'd treated Sharleen. Her words returned to him, played in his mind. Was there any truth to what she'd said? Could she help him manage his grief and discover his purpose in life? Or was she all talk? He considered going to her office to find out—and to apologize for his behavior on

Wednesday—but abandoned the thought. Who was he fooling? He didn't want to risk getting in a scuffle with the media hounds if he ventured outside of Greensboro. Plus, he didn't even know what he wanted to do with his life anymore. And he seriously doubted someone on his manager's payroll would give it to him straight.

Whistles went up in the lounge, drawing his attention to the front of the restaurant. His gaze fell on the statuesque woman in the waiting area and he felt his eyes widen. Emilio shook his head, but the image still remained. It was Sharleen Nichols.

Desire consumed him like wildfire.

Their eyes met, and a radiant smile exploded across her face. Sharleen waved in greeting, then strode purposely through the lounge, as if she owned the place. He straightened in his seat like a pupil at the head of the class. Narrowing his eyes, he zeroed in on his curvy, moving target. His heart revved louder than an engine, and an erection hardened inside his dark blue jeans. Short of breath, sweating uncontrollably, he leaned forward in his chair. *She's even more beautiful than I remember. How is that possible?*

Emilio looked Sharleen over, gave his eyes permission to roam. She was fashionably dressed in a tunic blouse, straight-leg pants and black high heels. She moved with a poise and grace that belied her age. Her red eyeglasses brightened her face, made her stand out from everyone else in the room. The suits at the bar were drinking beer and talking trash, but when Sharleen walked by, they fell silent.

Before Emilio could gather himself, Sharleen was at his booth, sitting down across from him. She smelled of jasmine and seemed to glow from within. Her inner beauty shone through, instantly seizing his attention. He was stunned to see her, and it must have shown on his face, because her smile dimmed.

"It's wonderful seeing you again. How have you been?"

Emilio couldn't speak. There was something magnetic about Sharleen, something so captivating he couldn't get his bearings. His heart thundered in his ears, beat out of control. For the first time in his life, he was speechless, more nervous than he'd ever been.

"You don't remember me..." Disappointment flashed across her pretty oval face. "I'm Sharleen Nichols from Pathways Center. We met on Wednesday at your estate."

Emilio parted his lips and forced his mouth to move. "I remember you."

"You do?" Sharleen sighed in relief. "Thank God for small miracles!"

Her eyes twinkled when she laughed, and the effervescent sound made him smile. The sun had zapped his energy during his afternoon jog, but he suddenly felt invigorated, energized. Sharleen looked genuinely happy to see him, and the feeling was definitely mutual. He was a great judge of character, always had been, and he sensed Sharleen Nichols was a nice girl.

Yeah, a nice girl you want to do very *bad things with in bed!*

The thought excited him, caused blood to surge to his groin. Sharleen was in her twenties, likely the same age as his sister Francesca and inexperienced in the ways of the world. He sensed it, felt it. Bits and pieces of his conversation with Antwan on Wednesday morning resurfaced. Emilio didn't remember much, but he knew one thing for sure: his manager had the hots for her. And that was reason enough to keep his distance and his eyes off her perfect shape.

That's right, his conscience said. *Dial it back, dude. She belongs to someone else.*

"Where's Antwan?" Sharleen asked, glancing around the lounge. "Is he still at the bar?"

"No. He's not here yet."

Lines of confusion wrinkled her forehead. "But I just spoke to him. He said you guys were drinking beer and shooting the breeze."

Emilio heard his cell phone buzz and picked it up off the table. He read his newest text message, then held up his iPhone. "Antwan isn't coming. He's stuck at the office."

A frown marred her delicate facial features.

"I didn't know you were joining us tonight," he said, to fill the long, awkward silence that descended over the table. "How do you know Jamieson? Is he a client of yours?"

"You lost me." Looking more confused than ever, she slanted her head and folded her arms across her chest. "This is supposed to be a business dinner, not a booze fest with the guys. Right?"

Mulling over her words, he stroked the length of his jaw. The truth came to him in a flash, and his face hardened like stone. "Antwan set us up, and I bet he told the other guys to stay away." He was annoyed with Antwan, pissed that he'd been tricked, but he kept his temper in check. "He played me, and I never saw it coming."

"This is ridiculous." Sharleen took her iPhone out of her purse, dialed a number and put it to her ear. "Unbe-liev-a-ble. Now he isn't answering his phone. How convenient."

"I should have known better. This is the oldest trick in the book—"

A devilish gleam filled her eyes. "Let's drive to his office and egg the place!"

Emilio cracked up. He couldn't remember the last time he'd laughed so hard, or so long, and it felt damned good. There was nothing sexier than a woman with a wicked sense of humor, and Sharleen cracked jokes with the skill of a comedy heavyweight. She spoke expressively, with her eyes and her hands, and her energy made him sit up and take notice.

"Let me buy you a drink." Emilio tried to sound casual, but his heart was pounding so hard it drowned out the noise in the room.

He saw her eyes widen and smiled to show his sincerity.

"You want me to stay?"

Emilio tried to play it cool, but he was desperate for her to stay. Eating alone was depressing, and he didn't want the other patrons—especially the nosy, female ones watching him like a hawk—to join him if Sharleen left. "Antwan wants us to talk, so let's talk," he said. "I'm curious about you, and I'd like to hear more about your work."

"You don't know how happy I am to hear you say that. To get through to you, I thought I'd have to break into your estate and corner you in your home gym!"

Please do. An erotic image, one too hot for TV, flashed in his mind. Emilio wet his lips with his tongue and returned her gaze. His pulse was pounding, clanging in his ears like the Liberty Bell, and his breathing was labored. *I can see you now...naked...bent over my weight bench...legs spread wide open...rocking those hips—*

"This is going to be fun. I want to learn more about you and explain more about life coaching..."

Emilio's testosterone level soared to unimaginable heights. His reaction to Sharleen embarrassed him, made him realize he was long overdue for a good, hard screw. But suddenly there was only one woman he hungered for.

Forget it. You have a better chance of winning the Masters Golf Tournament than getting Sharleen into bed. And besides, she belongs to Antwan, not you.

"There you are, you sexy beast. I've been looking all over for you."

Emilio groaned. He didn't have to turn around to see whom the high-pitched voice belonged to. Hanging his head, he cursed under his breath in Italian. His sister must have told her roommate where he'd be, because Ginger Barnes showing up at his favorite sports bar was no coincidence. The British nanny was the most obnoxious person he'd ever met, and the more she propositioned him, the less he liked her. Ginger latched on to anyone with wealth and success, and he suspected she was using Francesca to get close to him. Not that it mattered; she didn't stand a chance in hell of becoming Mrs. Emilio Morretti.

Bitter memories infiltrated his thoughts. Back in the day, before his life fell apart, he would've slept with Ginger without a second thought. He'd hooked up with a wide assortment of beauties during his fifteen-year racing career. But he was a different man now. Older, wiser and more discerning about the opposite sex, he no longer felt pressured to live the playboy lifestyle. Sadly, it had taken the loss of his beloved nephew for him to learn the errors of his ways.

"Hi," he muttered, as he clenched his teeth. Emilio didn't hide his displeasure, didn't pretend he was happy to see her. He didn't want his plans with Sharleen to go to ruin, so the sooner he got rid of Ginger the better. "What are you doing here?"

She cocked her head in his direction and licked her thin red lips in an exaggerated fashion. "What do you mean? I *love* sports."

"Really?" Emilio didn't believe her, not for a minute. "What team does LeBron James play for?"

Ginger wrinkled her nose. "Who's LeBron James?"

Checkmate! Emilio sneaked a glance at Sharleen, saw a grin dimple her cheek and knew she was amused. He stood, took Sharleen's hand and helped her to her feet. Winking at her, he rested a hand on the curve of her lower back and leaned in close. He'd always preferred pretty, natural types, not high-maintenance divas, and as he glanced between the women he realized they weren't even in the same league. Sharleen was a bombshell, with brains and personality, and that was damned hot.

"Let's head upstairs," he proposed, gesturing to the second floor with a flick of his head. "It's crowded down here, and I want us to have some privacy."

Her eyes brightened, and a bashful smile claimed her lips. Emilio envisioned kissing her, but struck the thought from his mind. She was his manager's girl, and although he was attracted to her, he'd never do anything to screw over his longtime friend.

"Y-y-you're on a date?" Ginger stammered, her

voice an earsplitting squeak. A horrified expression covered her face. "I thought you were alone."

"See you around. Take care."

Ginger slid in front of him, thwarting his escape. "If you're free later, maybe you can meet up with me and Francesca at Magic City. We're going club hopping with some out-of-town friends, and we're planning to party the night away."

Emilio glared at her. "My sister doesn't go to strip clubs."

"Okay," she shot back, with a knowing smirk. "If you say so!"

Disgusted, he strode out of the lounge with Sharleen at his side. Ginger was a bad influence on his twenty-five-year-old sister, and as he marched past the open kitchen, he made a mental note to talk to Francesca about finding another roommate. Or better yet, moving back into his estate. The thought heartened him, lifted his spirits. He missed seeing his sister every day and liked the idea of her living under his roof again. Francesca was still struggling to cope with the loss of Lucca, but partying with a wild crowd wasn't the answer.

Do you blame her? Her only child died, his conscience shot back. *And you're a fine one to talk. Had your daily dose of scotch today?*

"I don't see anyone upstairs. I hope we don't get into trouble for seating ourselves."

Emilio surfaced from his thoughts. "Don't worry. I've got this."

"Are you sure we won't get in trouble with management?"

"I'm positive. Cross my heart and hope to die."

Sharleen burst out laughing, and his chest puffed

up with pride. He felt fired up, happier than a kid at SeaWorld.

"Everyone's staring at us," she whispered, a note of anxiety in her voice. "But I guess you're used to it, being a world-famous race-car driver and all."

"They're not staring at me." Emilio fixed his gaze on hers and spoke from the heart. "You're a light, Sharleen, and they're floored by your inner and outer beauty. You're the prettiest woman in the room, and everyone knows it."

Her eyes revealed nothing, but her lips held a shy smile. As they exited the main floor lounge, Emilio caught the envious glares of the other male patrons and tightened his hold around her waist. "Leave everything to me. I know what I'm doing."

Chapter 5

"Tell me more about your background."

To buy herself some time, Sharleen picked up her glass and tasted her diet cola. The cold, sweet liquid tickled her taste buds and coursed down her throat in a gush. It didn't help cool her body down. Her temperature continued to climb, and perspiration drenched her skin. Emilio Morretti—the race-car driver with the quiet, soft-spoken nature—was to blame for her symptoms. Had to be. Why *else* was her heart racing and her hormones raging out of control? It was hard to concentrate with Emilio around, impossible to think clearly. Every time their eyes met, Sharleen lost her train of thought. Like right now. Try as she might, she couldn't remember his question.

"Don't be shy." Emilio sat across from her at the small wooden table, cutting up his T-bone steak, his gaze never leaving her face. "You're a fascinating young woman, and I'm enjoying your company very much."

Me? Fascinating? Really? But I'm a nobody, just a regular girl. "Thanks, but I'm older than you think." Sharleen paused, debated whether to divulge the truth. Over the past hour, Emilio had asked her tons of personal questions but had revealed little about himself. To gain his trust, she spoke openly. "I'm twenty-seven, but to be honest, I feel decades older. Everyone says I have an old soul, and it's true. I love crocheting, vintage clothes and The Beatles."

"We're kindred souls, then."

"We are?" she asked. "You crochet, too?"

Emilio chuckled. "No, but I have every song The Beatles ever recorded and a vinyl record player as well."

"No way! Me too!"

"You should come over sometime and check out my music library. It's quite impressive."

His tone was free of arrogance, but Sharleen sensed his pride, felt it radiating off him in waves. "I'd be honored," she said, touched by the offer. "Thanks for the invitation."

"Drop by my estate whenever your schedule permits."

For some reason, the thought of being alone with Emilio at his mansion excited her. *Slow your roll, girl. He's a client, not your soul mate.* Sharleen didn't have a "type," never had, and often teased her girlfriends who had a boyfriend checklist. But as the night wore on, she realized Emilio was everything she wanted in a man, and more. He was one of a kind, in a class all by himself. Cultured, sophisticated and chivalrous, he made her feel emotions she'd never experienced before, and everything about him—his eyes, his boyish smile, his foreign accent—was a turn-on.

"Were you raised in Atlanta, or did you relocate like everyone else in this fine city?"

Struggling to keep a straight face, Sharleen raised her right hand, as if she were pledging allegiance to the flag, and said, "I'm a native. Scout's honor."

"Great. The next time I need a tour guide I know just who to call."

A witty retort tickled her tongue, but Sharleen slammed her mouth shut. She was supposed to be evaluating Emilio, not flirting with him.

The second floor was filled with flat-screen TVs, pool tables and leather couches, but only a handful of people were relaxing in the lounge. Sharleen preferred the intimate setting, liked that they were far away from the crowd. She didn't want to share Emilio with anyone, especially not the British bombshell in the eye-catching pink number downstairs. *I wish I could wear dresses, too, but I can't. Not with my—*

"How long have you been a life coach?" Emilio asked.

Sharleen dismissed her thoughts and put her utensils down on her empty plate. "Five years. I got hired at Pathways Center right out of college, and I've been there ever since."

"Have you always dreamed of being a life coach?"

"No, actually. When I was a kid I wanted to be a mechanic—"

"A mechanic?" he repeated, a bewildered look on his face. "Why?"

"My dad owned a repair shop, and by the time I was ten I was answering phones, making coffee for the staff and tinkering on old cars." Sadness overwhelmed her, but she pushed past her feelings and spoke in a clear, strong voice. "My aunties were up in arms when I started trade school, but my parents told me to ignore them. They encouraged me to follow my heart, and that's exactly what I did."

Emilio frowned. "If your dream was to follow in your father's footsteps, then why are you a life coach and not a mechanic?"

Sharleen opened her mouth, but her throat ached, and it hurt to swallow. She'd told her story hundreds of times over the years, everywhere from churches to schools and youth centers, but when she remembered that cold winter night, her vision blurred with unshed tears, and the room spun. She sipped water to help steady her nerves and focus her thoughts. "My parents died in a house fire when I was seventeen," she said. "I gave up on life and quit school."

"I am sorry for your loss." Emilio placed a hand on hers and held it tight. His touch was welcome, and his eyes were full of sympathy. "Unfortunately, I know how you feel. After my nephew died, I didn't have the strength to get out of bed, let alone go out in public."

They sat in silence for a long moment, alone with their thoughts. The waitress arrived, cleared their empty dinner plates without saying a word and sped off.

"I never would have guessed you experienced such a devastating loss," Emilio said quietly. "You're so bright and bubbly and passionate about life."

It wasn't always that way. I wanted to die when I woke up in the hospital.

"How did you survive losing your parents? How did you overcome your grief?"

"In the most unlikely way." Dropping her hands in her lap, she fiddled with her silver gemstone bracelet. It had belonged to her mother, and although it was nicked and scratched, Sharleen wore it every day. It was her good-luck charm, the only piece of jewelry she owned, and her most valuable possession. "I moved in with my aunt Phyllis, and after months of me moping around the house, complaining about how unfair life was, she let me have it—"

"That's terrible." Emilio's face darkened, and there was a bitter edge to his voice. "How could she turn on you in your time of need? You were grieving the loss of your parents—"

"And squandering my life away," Sharleen explained, feeling compelled to defend her favorite aunt. "I stormed out of the apartment in a huff, but deep down I knew my aunt Phyllis was right. My parents wouldn't want me wasting away to nothing. They'd want me to make something of myself, and that's what I'm striving to do."

His gaze bored into her, zeroing in with acute precision. Sharleen never imagined their lighthearted conversation would turn into a serious, soul-baring discussion. She took a moment to catch her breath. Antwan's words came back to her. *Treat Emilio like a friend, not a patient. Be his confidante. Someone he can trust.* This was her moment to get through to him, to use her personal story to reach him, and she wasn't going to squander the opportunity. "The way I see it, you have two choices.

You can either heal or allow grief to consume you. It's as simple as that."

He lowered his head, dropped his gaze to his lap.

"If I can overcome the pain of my past, then you can, too. I promise to be there to help you every step of the way, Emilio. You can do this." Sharleen raised an index finger. "Give me a month. If after thirty days, you still think I'm full of it, I'll give Antwan a refund."

"That won't be necessary. Antwan says you're worth every penny, and I believe him. We've only been talking for a few hours, but I'm already impressed."

So am I. You're kind and sweet and *fine as hell!*

"I'm not averse to counseling, but I can't come to your office." He shrugged and gave a small smile. "I can't risk the paparazzi or my family finding out that I'm in therapy. My cousins and brothers would tease me mercilessly."

"How many siblings do you have?"

"Hell if I know," he said, with a wry laugh. "My father's been married four times, and I lost count of how many siblings I had years ago!"

Emilio chuckled, and Sharleen did, too.

"I'm kidding. I have six brothers and two sisters. My old man loves kids and thinks having them around keeps him young, so I wouldn't be surprised if he decided to have more children!"

The waitress, who was clearly a college student trying to pay her way through school, arrived with the bill.

Emilio took out his wallet, slid his platinum card through the portable debit machine and punched in his PIN. "Thanks for everything, miss. The food was great."

The waitress retrieved the machine and cupped a

hand over her mouth. "A thousand-dollar tip?" she shrieked. "This is awesome. Thank you so much!"

Sharleen was impressed by Emilio's generosity, but she wondered if it was all for show. Did he give the waitress a huge tip just to impress her? Or was this just another day in the life of a superstar athlete worth millions? Watching him with growing interest, she felt enthralled by him—and aroused, too. It wasn't every day she met a sensitive, thoughtful guy with a big heart. *No wonder I'm hot for him. Who wouldn't be? He's every woman's dream man!*

"It's time to switch gears."

Emilio stood, came around the table and helped Sharleen out of her chair.

"Let's have another round of drinks and play pool."

"I hate to brag, but I won several pool tournaments in college."

"Famous last words…"

"Want to bet?" An idea came to mind and a smile filled her lips. "If I win, you're going to be my guest at the Mind, Body & Soul Conference this weekend—"

"And if I win you're going to be my live-in chef for the rest of the month."

As if! Sharleen made her eyes wide, as if she were shocked, but she was secretly amused.

"I love Southern cuisine, and the pictures of your bayou fried shrimp and coconut cream pie look delicious." He moved closer, swallowed the space between them. "Can I get a taste?"

Anytime, anyplace. His voice tickled the tips of her ears. His gaze held her captive, awakened every cell in her body. Sharleen stood as still as stone, but her heart was pounding inside her chest, racing erratically.

"What were you doing poking around my Instagram page?"

"Just doing my research."

Sharleen felt a glimmer of pride when she caught Emilio steal a peek at her butt, but she pretended not to notice. In the arcade, she selected a cue stick, gripped it in a loose, relaxed manner and hit the cue ball so hard it shot down the pool table at lightning-fast speed.

Ten minutes into the game, Sharleen realized Emilio had no hope of beating her. He was more interested in shooting the breeze with her than playing the game. He asked dozens of questions about her family and career life, and the more they talked, the less tense he seemed, the more relaxed. He was lowering his guard, finally opening up to her, and she was thrilled they were finally getting along. They chatted effortlessly about current topics, their favorite hobbies and activities, and swapped hilarious stories about their childhoods.

"Tell me something about you that no one else knows."

Sharleen shook her head. "You first."

"That's easy. I'm addicted to golf, ESPN and the video game 'Need for Speed,' of course." He reached out and touched a hand to her cheek. "*And* I have a weakness for women who wear red glasses."

"Sure you do. And I love men with long, curly chest hair!"

Emilio laughed, and her heart soared. Sharleen didn't know if he was flirting with her just for the hell of it or because he was genuinely attracted to her, but she enjoyed his attention. Although, she wasn't a gullible fool—she knew better than to take him seriously.

Relationships didn't work, and love didn't last. Screw

their attraction and mind-blowing chemistry. A superstar athlete with legions of female fans couldn't be
trusted, so falling for Emilio was out of the question.

"If I score here the game is over."

Emilio cocked an eyebrow and held up his palms.
"What, no trick shot?"

"If you insist." Sharleen slid her pool stick behind
her back and lowered her hips as if she were doing the
limbo. "Nine ball, corner pocket."

Holding her breath, Sharleen watched as the cue ball
bounced off the rails, sped down the table and dropped
into the corner pocket. Thrilled about her win, she
danced around the pool table and laughed when the
other patrons on the second floor broke into applause.

"Congratulations."

"Why, thank you, Mr. Morretti."

The epitome of cool, he leaned against the table and
crossed his legs at the ankles. "You're a great player,
Ms. Nichols. And beautiful, too."

Scared she was going to fall victim to her desire,
Sharleen tore her gaze away from his mouth and sipped
her drink.

"I thought the World Series Racing fans were zeal-
ous, but they've got nothing on you!" he said.

"Do you miss racing?"

"Promise you won't tell Antwan?"

Sharleen nodded, instinctively moving toward him.
She narrowed her eyes, locked in on him, and everyone else in the room faded to the background. "You
have my word."

"Racing is in my blood. It's what I was born to do.
And I feel incomplete without it."

"Then why don't you enter the All-Star Race?"

His tone was filled with skepticism. "What do *you* know about the All-Star Race?"

"I know you won the event three consecutive times, *and* that your last record-breaking win cemented your place in the Hall of Fame," Sharleen said, glad she'd done her research. "You're a global icon, with legions of fans, and the league just isn't the same without you."

Smiling politely, he bowed his head. "You're giving me too much credit."

"I think you're being modest."

"A lot of people had a hand in my professional accomplishments. I had an awesome run and incredible success, but none of it would have happened without the support of my family, my sponsors and my loyal, hardworking pit crew..."

Having coached high-profile clients with monster-size egos before, Sharleen was surprised by Emilio's humility. He wasn't trying to impress her or putting on airs; he was speaking from the heart, and it was obvious he meant every word he said.

"I dream about returning to the sport almost every day," he confessed. "I miss the competition, traveling to exotic locales and most importantly—"

"The groupies at every pit stop?"

Sharleen regretted the words the moment they left her mouth. His furrowed eyebrows and clenched jaw told her he was put off by her joke. "I'm sorry," she said, smiling apologetically. "I didn't mean to interrupt you. Please continue."

"I miss my crew. Those guys are my brothers, and I think about them all the time."

"You should give them a call."

"I can't. After my nephew died, I pushed them away..."

Emilio sighed then shrugged. "I want to reach out, but I don't know what to say."

"'Hello. How are you?' is a pretty good place to start."

A grin dimpled his cheek. "You have all the answers, don't you?"

To keep the mood light and playful, Sharleen joked, "Yes, as a matter of fact, I do!"

"I'm glad we met." He tipped his head toward her and dropped his voice to a low, throaty pitch. "You're the kind of woman I need in my life."

Your professional life or your personal life?

Sharleen didn't know how it happened, but they were side by side. Their arms were touching, their legs, too, and they were so close she could see the rise and fall of his chest. "Can I give you a piece of advice? Something my father used to tell me?"

He nodded his head and stared at her.

Her body was trembling, but she conquered her nerves and spoke in a clear, confident voice. "It doesn't matter what people say or think about you. Do what brings you joy, and always be your true, authentic self. At the end of the day, that is really all that matters."

"Your father was a wise man, and it's obvious you inherited his remarkable insight."

His words were kind, and his eyes were full of sympathy, but she became flustered nonetheless. He was out-and-out flirting with her, and it felt great! Her emotions seesawed between excitement and trepidation. Emilio was a good guy, an honest-to-goodness gentleman, and the more they talked, the more Sharleen desired him. *I am in* way *over my head. Maybe I should refer Emilio to Brad—*

"Do you like live music?" he asked, giving her forearm an affectionate squeeze. "There's a jazz café a few blocks from here, and the house band is one of the best I've ever heard."

"I'd better not. It's almost midnight, and tomorrow's going to be a long, busy day." Remembering their bet, Sharleen picked up her purse and took out a glossy white brochure. "There are tons of free workshops offered at the conference, but I highly recommend Stress Less, Live More; Life Plans for Dummies, and Reclaim Your Life Today."

"You're going to hold me to our bet, aren't you?"

"Absolutely!"

Emilio took the brochure and looked it over. "Interesting."

Sharleen expected him to make excuses for why he couldn't attend the event, but to her surprise he said, "I'll be there. When and where should we meet?"

"I'll meet you at the front entrance of the convention center at one o'clock."

"Don't make any plans for dinner, because after the conference I'm taking you to Dolce Vita Atlanta for the culinary experience of a lifetime."

"I *love* that restaurant. It's a date."

Sharleen finally felt confident that she could help Emilio overcome the pain of his past—but she just had to do it without losing her dignity and self-respect. *Just because I'm attracted to Emilio doesn't mean I can't effectively do my job. Besides, if Brad can socialize with clients after dark, so can I!*

"I had a great time tonight. This was fun," Emilio said.

"This was nothing," she quipped, dismissing his

words with a wave of her hand. "You're going to have even *more* fun at the Mind, Body & Soul Conference tomorrow."

Emilio gave a hearty laugh. "I'll walk you to your car."

He took her hand, led her down the staircase and through the empty lounge. Outside, the streets were loud and crowded. The moon hung high in the sky, the air smelled sweet and the wind whistled through the trees. It was the perfect night for stargazing, for cuddling with that special someone in bed, and Sharleen secretly wished she had someone special in her life, a man who would love her in spite of her—

"Thanks for dinner *and* that nail-biting pool game."

Sharleen playfully poked his shoulder. "Don't hate 'cause I'm fabulous!"

"*That* you are." Emilio dropped a kiss on her cheek. "Drive home safe."

"I'll see you tomorrow."

"You can count on it."

He opened the driver's-side door for her and stepped aside. "Good night."

Sharleen started the engine, waved and drove slowly through the parking lot. In the rearview mirror, she watched Emilio hop into the gleaming white sports car parked in front of the bar. Her temperature rose, and desire burned hot inside her. She needed a stiff drink and a cold shower, or it was going to be a *very* long night.

Chapter 6

"Sweetie, open up. It's me." Sharleen pressed her palms against the window, stood on her tiptoes and peered inside the quaint brick house. Spotting a figure curled up on the couch, she banged on the glass until her hands throbbed with pain. "Jocelyn, I *know* you're home, and I'm not leaving until we talk, so get up and open the door!"

Remembering where she was, Sharleen straightened and smoothed a hand over her ivory blouse. Faking a smile, she waved at the elderly woman walking her poodles. Jocelyn lived in Grant Park, a working-class neighborhood filled with professionals, families and retirees, and Sharleen feared if she continued banging on the window, one of Jocelyn's neighbors would call the cops, and she'd be arrested for trespassing.

Frustrated, she crossed her arms and tapped her foot impatiently on the ground. Sharleen knew Jocelyn was upset about being fired, but she was taking things too far. She wasn't answering her cell phone or responding to her text messages, and now she was blatantly ignoring her. *What's up with that? Why is she pushing me away? We're* supposed *to be girls.*

To calm herself down, she counted to ten and inhaled a deep breath. As Sharleen stood on the porch, contemplating her next move, her thoughts turned to Emilio.

Her mood instantly brightened, and a smile warmed her lips. They'd had a great time last night, and although Sharleen was annoyed with Antwan for tricking her, she'd enjoyed the one-on-one time with Emilio. He'd opened up to her, agreed to meet her at the Mind, Body & Soul Conference that afternoon and even promised to take her out for dinner. And that morning, as she was eating breakfast, he'd surprised her with a hilarious text message.

Can I have a picture of you, so I can show Santa what I want for Christmas?

She'd laughed so hard soy milk had spewed out of her mouth. For the past two hours, they'd been trading text messages, and every time his name popped up on her cell-phone screen her heart danced with excitement. *Working with Emilio is going to be a challenge, but I know I can do it. I have to, or Brad will swoop in and steal him away—*

The front door creaked open. Sharleen felt her mouth fall open, but she quickly shut it. Jocelyn, the biracial cutie with the quick wit and flamboyant personality, was a mess. Her yellow bathrobe was wrinkled, stained with coffee, and her curly brown hair was disheveled. She looked exhausted, as if she hadn't slept in weeks, and she was nervously shuffling her feet.

"Jocelyn, how are you?" Sharleen knew it was a dumb question, regretted it the moment the words left her mouth, but she didn't know what else to say. "Are you okay?"

"I'm fine. What are you doing here?"

"Now, is that any way to greet your partner in crime?" Sharleen asked, giving her best friend a hug. "I haven't heard from you in a few days, and I got worried. It's not like you to ignore my calls, so I decided to stop by for a visit."

"I have a lot on my mind," she mumbled. "I'm busy. You should go."

Ignoring her, Sharleen walked inside the house and kicked off her sandals. Glancing around the kitchen, she was shocked to see dishes piled high in the sink, the hardwood floors streaked with dirt and the over-flowing garbage can.

Sharleen opened the fridge, grabbed everything she needed to make breakfast and placed the ingredients on the granite countertop. "Sit," she said, pointing at the table. "I'm making you a Sante Fe omelet, and you're going to love it."

"Don't bother." Jocelyn dropped into a chair. "I'm not hungry."

"When was the last time you ate?"

"Can't remember."

Sharleen washed the vegetables, chopped them up and tossed them in a glass bowl. "How's your mom doing? Has she been discharged from the hospital?"

"No, they're running additional tests and prepping her for surgery."

"Try not to worry. Your mom's a fighter. She'll pull through."

To reassure her, Sharleen squeezed her hand. Jocelyn had taken Sharleen under her wing when she started working at Pathways, and over the years they'd become closer than sisters. They had weekly girls' nights, traveled together and spent holidays with Jocelyn's fun-loving Bahamian family. After numerous visits to the ER, Mrs. Calhoun had been diagnosed with heart failure, but her cardiologist was confident her upcoming surgery would be a success.

"When are you going to the hospital?" Sharleen turned on the stove, sprayed the frying pan with cooking oil and poured in the egg batter. "If it's okay, I'd like to come with you."

Her face brightened. "My mom would love that. She asks about you all the time."

"Think I can get away with sneaking food into the hospital for her?"

"If you do, she'll love you even more!"

"Then it's worth the risk." Sharleen pointed the spatula at Jocelyn. "But if I get arrested you *better* bail me out ASAP, or else."

The joke lightened the mood, caused the tension in the air to recede.

"Aren't you supposed to be at the Mind, Body & Soul Conference?" Jocelyn asked.

"I wanted to check in on you, so I switched time slots with Christelle."

Jocelyn's cell phone buzzed, and she glanced down at the screen. "Men are jerks," she fumed. "They're dogs who can't be trusted, and we're better off without them."

Not all of them, Sharleen thought. Emilio had a gentle nature, and she felt close to him, connected to him in a way she'd never experienced before. What was it he'd said? *You're the prettiest woman in the room... I had a great time with you tonight... Don't make any plans for dinner. I'm taking you to Dolce Vita Atlanta for the culinary experience of a lifetime.*

"I wish I could get away for a while." Jocelyn picked up a pack of cigarettes off the table and opened it. "If my mom wasn't sick, that's exactly what I'd do."

"You quit smoking, remember?"

"I'm stressed. I need something to help calm my nerves."

"Then I'll fix you a cup of coffee." Sharleen snatched the lighter out of Jocelyn's hand and stuffed it inside her back pocket. "Friends don't let friends smoke."

"I *really* wish you'd leave. I'm not in the mood for your mouth today…"

Pretending she didn't hear her, Sharleen returned to the stove, whistling a tune. Arguing with Jocelyn would only make the situation worse, so she finished cooking breakfast and pretended not to notice her best friend glaring at her. Minutes later, she put the omelet on a plate, set it down on the table and said with a smile, "Bon appétit."

Jocelyn stared longingly at the pack of cigarettes.

"Eat. You'll feel better."

"Quit bossing me around," she snapped.

I wouldn't have to if you weren't acting like such a drama queen. Deciding to give Jocelyn space, she returned to the sink and put on rubber gloves. Sharleen loaded the dishwasher, swept the floor and emptied the garbage, all the while thinking about Emilio. It was hard not to. There was something about him that appealed to her, that touched her in a profound way, and she was looking forward to meeting up with him at the conference that afternoon. "Here's your coffee," Sharleen said, putting the ceramic mug on the table.

"Sorry for snapping at you, but I'm having the day from hell."

"Do you want to talk about it?"

Jocelyn shrugged. "What's there to talk about? My life is ruined."

"There are other jobs and tons of great coaching centers right here in Atlanta."

"I shouldn't have trusted Brad." Her voice wobbled, cracked with emotion. "How could I have been so stupid? So desperate that I didn't realize he was playing me?"

Frowning, Sharleen sat down. "What does Brad have to do with you getting fired?"

"I don't want to talk about it. It's too embarrassing."

"We're friends. You can trust me."

Jocelyn lowered her eyes to the floor and hugged her legs to her chest.

"I'd never betray you. You know that."

"I…" She stumbled over her words and paused to gather herself. "I slept with Brad."

"No! Why? You hate him more than I do!"

"I know, but he showed up here with flowers and Chinese takeout on my birthday, and I caved. I was lonely, and for a while he helped me forget my problems."

Guilt consumed Sharleen, made her feel low. This

was all her fault. If she'd spent last Monday night with Jocelyn, instead of working late, her friend wouldn't be in a miserable funk now. She'd make it up to her, would spare no expense. They were tighter than Gayle and Oprah, and Sharleen knew just what to do to lift her spirits. Front-row seats to the Rashad J concert were going to set her back hundreds of dollars, but Jocelyn was worth it. "You're fabulous, and don't let anyone tell you otherwise, especially that louse Brad."

"I know, but I thought I'd be married with two or three kids by now."

Sharleen didn't know what to say. They'd had this conversation countless times before, as recently as last week, but nothing she said ever made Jocelyn feel better. So she just smiled sympathetically and nodded her head at the appropriate junctures.

"I don't expect you to understand. You're still in your twenties."

"You're right," Sharleen conceded, determined not to argue with her best friend. "I don't understand why you're freaked about getting older, or why finding a husband is so important to you, but sleeping with Brad isn't the answer. Hooking up with a colleague is asking for trouble."

"You can say that again. He's a sloppy kisser, a selfish lover and a lousy lay."

"I'm not surprised. He's got small feet *and* a huge ego!"

Jocelyn laughed, but the lighthearted reprieve didn't last long. Sadness clouded her features, and her shoulders sagged under the weight of her despair. "Brad cornered me in the staff room the next day, and when I refused to give him a blow job, he went off on me."

"What a pig," Sharleen scoffed, disgusted. "He used to be a decent guy, but he changed when he got his master certification last fall. Unfortunately, he let success go to his head."

Silence fell over the room, and when Jocelyn finally spoke, her voice was strained with anguish. "Brad threatened me." Her eyes filled with tears, and her lips trembled. "He said if I make trouble for him with Mrs. Fontaine, he'll post naked pictures of me online."

"Jocelyn, ignore him. He's bluffing."

"No…he's not… He has pictures of me on his iPhone."

"They're fakes," Sharleen insisted. "People alter photographs all the time."

"They're real. It's definitely me. He must have taken them when I fell asleep."

Anger rose inside her, and as Sharleen listened to Jocelyn's story unfold, she found it hard to control her temper. No wonder her friend was holed up inside the house, crying her eyes out; Brad was threatening to ruin her life. Jocelyn looked terrified, scared out of her mind, and for good reason. Brad McClendon was a lying, scheming manipulator who preyed on lonely women, and there was no telling what he'd do next.

"I don't know how much more of this I can take. He's been calling and texting me nonstop, and I'm sick of it. I'm so stressed-out, I feel like I'm losing my mind."

A cold wind whipped through the kitchen, and a shiver zipped down Sharleen's spine. The situation was worse than she'd thought. She had to act; she had to do something, but what? *Should I confront Brad with what I know or go straight to Mrs. Fontaine?* The answer eluded her, and the more she thought about it, the more confused she was.

"I still can't believe this is happening. I played right into his hands…"

To comfort her, Sharleen rubbed her shoulders. Watching Jocelyn, seeing the anguished expression on her face, brought tears to her eyes. In all the years they'd been friends, she'd never seen her like this. Never, not once, not even when her fiancé broke things off last year. "This is wrong. We can't let Brad get away with this."

Jocelyn kept her head down, didn't look at her or respond.

"We have to go to Mrs. Fontaine and tell her what happened."

"I already did. She didn't believe me."

"What?" exploded out of her mouth in a deafening shout. "Why not?"

"Because Brad met with her *first* and accused me of propositioning him at work."

Sharleen gasped. "He didn't!"

"Mrs. Fontaine fired me, and when I turned in my keys, she said if I try and contact any of my clients, she'll sue me for breach of contract. Can she do that?"

"Yes, unfortunately, she can."

Jocelyn sniffed and wiped her nose with the sleeve of her bathrobe. "This couldn't have happened at a worse time. I *just* signed Zoe Archer-Ross—"

"The actress? I didn't know you were working with her."

"I was hired to be her sober coach," she explained. "I balked when her agent first contacted me, but when he told me the studio would triple my hourly rate, I said *hell yeah*."

"Twelve hundred dollars a day is fantastic money. You'd be a fool to turn that down."

"I was planning to use that money to pay off my mom's medical bills..." Her face crumpled, and tears spilled down her cheeks. "What am I going to do? She's counting on me."

Sharleen took Jocelyn in her arms and held her tight. She hated to see her cry, and her own eyes teared up as she listened to Jocelyn sob. She felt defeated, as helpless as a child, but she tried to speak with confidence. "Don't worry," she said calmly. "Everything will be fine. I promise."

"How? Brad's crazy, and Mrs. Fontaine turned her back on me."

"We'll get through this together." Sharleen didn't recognize her own voice and feared she was going to break down, too. Pulling herself together, she cleared her throat and forced a smile. "I love you, but if you don't quit drooling on my Versace blouse I'm out of here!"

Jocelyn laughed through her tears. "Sorry about that."

"No worries. You can buy me another one when you get a fabulous new coaching gig."

"Do you think I'll get hired on at another agency?"

"I don't think. *I know*," she said, with a fervent nod. "You're an amazing life coach and a savvy business-woman. It's just a matter of time before you get another job. I'm sure of it."

Pride filled Jocelyn's eyes. "I'm going to go take a shower and get dressed."

Sharleen plugged her nose with one hand and waved

the other in front of her face. "Good idea, girlfriend. You stink!"

Wearing a bashful smile, Jocelyn stood and shuffled down the hallway.

Brad messed with the wrong woman, and I'm going to make him pay! A plan began to formulate in her mind. Sharleen knew what she had to do. She had to get the VP job. It was the answer to her problems, the only way to get rid of Brad "The Snake" McClendon once and for all.

Sharleen envisioned herself signing her new employment contract, moving into the large corner office with the cushy furniture and showing her arch nemesis to the door. The image heartened her, made her more determined than ever to beat Brad at his own game. Because once she was vice president of Pathways Center, she was going to find a way to get rid of Brad and rehire Jocelyn. For the first time since arriving at the house, Sharleen felt as if everything was going to be okay.

Chapter 7

Sharleen spotted Brad at the Pathways Center booth inside the Atlanta Convention Center and narrowed her eyes in disgust. He was nothing to write home about, but what he lacked in the looks department, he more than made up for in personality. He was great with people, especially the opposite sex. Women were gathered around the booth, batting their eyelashes and gazing adoringly at him, as if he were the man of their dreams.

More like a nightmare with dimples!

The sound of his loud, hearty chuckle made her skin crawl. She wanted to knee Brad in the groin for what he'd done to Jocelyn, but lashing out at her colleague—and her boss's favorite employee—would only make the situation worse. Now, more than ever, she needed to keep a cool head. By the time Sharleen reached the booth Brad was alone, typing on his iPhone. The moment he saw her, he jumped to his feet and shoved his cell into his back pocket.

"Hey," she said, forcing the word out through pursed lips.

"There you are. I've been waiting to see your pretty face." Brad glanced over his shoulder and licked his lips. "And that fat, juicy ass."

Sharleen glared at him. "What did you say?"

"Cool your heels. It was a compliment."

"Keep your compliments to yourself. I don't need them."

"FYI," he said, with a wink. "I like when you're feisty. It's a turn-on."

Taking a giant step back, Sharleen reached into her purse, took out a pack of breath mints and shoved it into his hands. "Here. Take this. I insist."

His eyes darkened. "You think you're hot stuff because you graduated from Duke, but I'm not impressed. You're a second-rate life coach and everyone knows it."

Sharleen let his insult roll off her back and smiled brightly at everyone who passed their booth.

"It's too bad about Jocelyn getting canned, huh? In my opinion, it was long overdue…"

Her eyes thinned, and her temper flared. Sharleen wanted to strangle Brad, to kill him with her bare hands. She imagined how good it would feel wringing his scrawny neck.

"Have you spoken to Jocelyn recently?"

Sharleen ignored the question, pretended she didn't hear it. "'Bye, Brad. See you around."

"I'm not going anywhere. I'm here for the rest of the day. Boss's orders."

"All Pathways employees are entitled to man the

booth for an hour," she reminded him. "This is my time
to hand out business cards and sign up new clients."

"You were supposed to be here from nine to ten."

"I switched time slots with Christelle."

"Too bad," he said, with a dismissive shrug of his
shoulders. "You snooze, you lose."

"I can't believe this. You're incredible—"

"Thanks, toots, you're not too bad yourself, *and* you
have a great rack…" He broke off speaking, and the
lewd grin slid off his face. "It's an honor to meet you,
Mr. Morretti. I'm Brad McClendon, one of the Master
Life Coaches at Pathways Center…"

Sharleen turned around, saw Emilio standing behind her and swallowed a moan. He smelled of expensive cologne and looked fantastic in his tan sports
coat, crisp white shirt and blue jeans. Sharleen would
never have an affair with a client, but dammit if she
wasn't tempted. She wondered what his lips tasted like,
longed to caress his handsome face and broad, muscled
shoulders. Her attraction to Emilio was all-consuming,
so powerful her body throbbed with need. The Italian
race-car driver was an international superstar, but he
was more than just another rich, hot athlete. He was a
sweet, gentle soul. That was damned sexy, appealing
in every way. But what impressed Sharleen most about
Emilio was his quiet confidence. He had zero ego, and
he treated everyone he met with kindness and respect.

"I was hoping I'd find you here."

*Don't just stand there like a bump on a log. Speak,
dammit, speak!* All she could think about was kissing
him, tasting his lips once and for all. But she wiped the
thought from her mind and found her voice. "Hi, Emilio.
How are you?"

"Great, now that I've found you."

"Are you enjoying the conference so far?"

"Yes, as a matter of fact, I am. Thanks for inviting me." He looked at her with a thoughtful expression. "The Stress Less, Live More workshop starts in fifteen minutes, and I was hoping you'd join me."

Before Sharleen could respond, Brad stepped in front of her and vigorously shook Emilio's hand. "I'm your biggest fan," he boasted, with a wide, toothy smile. "I've worked with dozens of high-profile celebrities over the past nine years, and I think we'd be a perfect fit."

"I already have a life coach, and the fact that I'm here proves how persuasive she is."

Brad chuckled, but it sounded forced. "You're in good hands."

"I couldn't have said it better myself." Emilio gave a curt nod. "See you around, Chad."

Sharleen wanted to laugh in "Chad"'s face. But she remembered the heartbreaking conversation she'd had that morning with Jocelyn and bit the inside of her cheek to stifle her giggles. They walked through the convention center, out into the lobby and stopped in front of the elevators. "Did you mean what you just said about me being your life coach?"

"Yes, but only if you agree to my terms."

"They are?" she prompted.

"I would like us to do our sessions at my estate."

Sharleen mulled over his words, then slowly nodded her head. "I'm fine with that, and as long as you're open and receptive to my coaching methods, we'll get along great."

"How many sessions do you recommend a week?"

"We can do as few as one or as many as five. It's up to you."

"Five sounds good."

His words made her head spin. *Three days ago Emilio threw me out of his estate, and now he wants me to be his life coach. Miracles really* do *happen!* Sharleen liked the idea of seeing him every day and was excited about working with him. Who wouldn't be? He was easy to talk to, the most down-to-earth celebrity she'd ever met and a great conversationalist. Sharleen had high hopes for Emilio and was confident she could help him conquer his grief.

"I'd like to do our sessions during my morning workout. Is that cool with you?"

"Absolutely." His smile stirred her hormones, made her temperature rise, but she maintained her composure. "Are there any other terms I need to know about?"

"I'll introduce you as my girlfriend to my friends and family, not my life coach."

Her displeasure must have shown on her face, because he said, "Is that a problem?"

"Emilio, I won't pretend to be something I'm not. That goes against what I believe."

"I feel strongly about protecting my privacy and keeping my personal life out of the tabloids," he countered, glancing around the lobby. "Those are my conditions. Take it or leave it."

A one-liner shot out of her mouth. "How can I refuse when you asked so nicely?"

Emilio fixed his eyes on hers and licked his lips with deliberate slowness, as if he were trying to arouse her. It worked. Her body was on fire, hot with lust. Sharleen sensed his interest in her and their growing attraction, but ignored her feelings. Nothing good could come out of them having a sexual relationship.

Ha! As if things would ever *get that far. You're so scared of rejection, you've sabotaged all of your relationships—*

"I'm sorry. I didn't mean to snap at you," Emilio said.

"I'll let it slide this time, but don't let it happen again."

Amusement gleamed in his eyes. "I wouldn't dream of it."

"I'm a life coach, not a human doormat, and don't you forget it."

Emilio chuckled. "Now that you've given me a thorough tongue-lashing, I'd like to head to the workshop. The quicker we finish up here, the quicker we can go eat!"

Sharleen and Emilio were sitting outside talking on the patio at Dolce Vita Atlanta, when the waiter hustled over to their table.

"I apologize for the delay in bringing your desserts, but the Hawks game just ended, and it's jam-packed inside."

"No worries," Emilio said good-naturedly to the waiter. "I'm having such a great time with my beautiful dinner companion, I forgot all about dessert."

"I wish *I* could be so lucky!" the young waiter said.

Emilio addressed the waiter, but he stared at Sharleen with longing in his eyes. "It's hard to find a good woman, so when you find that special someone, don't let her go."

The heat of his gaze made her mouth dry and her

skin tingle. *The sexiest athlete on the planet is flirting with me. I* must *be dreaming!* Sharleen needed a moment to catch her breath, so she sipped her cocktail. Reflecting on her favorite parts of the day made her smile. After the Stress Less, Live More workshop, they'd chatted with the keynote speaker, checked out the various vendor booths and enjoyed lattes in the lobby café.

Driving to Dolce Vita Atlanta in Emilio's Bugatti had been an exhilarating ride, but nothing compared to entering the celebrity hot spot on his arm. Stylish and elegant, Dolce Vita was known for its outstanding food, excellent service and moneyed clientele. They were given the royal treatment, and when they sat down on the patio, waiters rushed over carrying trays filled with caviar and cocktails. Dinner had been a scrumptious feast and their conversation lively and fun. Attentive and sweet, Emilio asked poignant questions about life coaching and proposed a toast to their new friendship.

Sharleen fanned a hand to her face. An umbrella shielded the booth from the sun, a lavish flower arrangement dressed the table and lanterns cast a soft glow around the patio.

"The peach cobbler was an excellent choice. It's one of my favorites."

The waiter had a goofy expression on his face and was staring adoringly at Sharleen.

"Thanks," Emilio said curtly. "We'll let you know if we need anything else."

The waiter didn't move. Sharleen felt uncomfortable, as if she were under a microscope. But when Emilio squeezed her hand, her anxiety disappeared. She liked when he touched her, couldn't get enough of his gentle caress. She felt as if her mind and body disconnected whenever he was around. *Get it together. You're a successful, accomplished woman. Not a tween girl on her first date!*

"I don't mean to be rude, but we'd like to have some privacy."

"Yes, of course, Mr. Morretti." Smiling sheepishly, the waiter gave a polite nod. "Enjoy your dessert, miss. I'll be back in a few minutes to check on you."

The waiter left, and Emilio grinned broadly. "Finally. I thought he'd never leave!"

Laughing, Sharleen picked up her fork and cut into her peach cobbler.

"The waiter definitely likes you."

She scoffed and rolled her eyes.

"Can't say I blame him, though. You're stunning."

"Why would he be interested in me?" she asked, ignoring his compliment. "I'm a businesswoman, not a bombshell."

"Are you saying businesswomen can't be sexy?"

No. But I'm not.

"Intelligence and confidence are what makes a woman irresistible, and you possess both qualities in spades." His voice deepened, dropped to a husky whisper. "You're unlike anyone I've ever met, and the more time we spend together the more I'm attracted to you."

Sharleen forced herself to keep her mouth shut, told herself not to indulge him. Flirting with a client was never a good idea, and since she didn't want Emilio to think she had feelings for him, she dodged his gaze and continued eating her dessert.

"How long have you been dating Antwan?"

Sharleen choked on her peach cobbler. To alleviate

the burning sensation in her chest, she picked up her glass and sipped her drink. "Antwan and I are friends, and nothing more," she said. "He's like the brother I never had."

"That's great news—" His phone buzzed in his pocket, and he fished it out and stared at the screen. "It's my sister. Do you mind?"

"No, not at all. Take as long as you need."

"Ciao, Francesca. *Che succede? Tutto bene?"*

While Emilio was on the phone, Sharleen sent Jocelyn a text message. She hadn't heard from her friend all day and wanted to see if she was okay. Shielding her eyes from the sun, Sharleen sank back against the plush cushions and crossed her legs.

Sharleen's gaze fell on Emilio, and she spent several minutes examining his strong facial features. He spoke in Italian, but his furrowed eyebrows and clipped tone suggested he was angry. Ending his call, he dropped his iPhone on the table.

"Is everything okay?"

"Sometimes I feel like a human ATM machine," he complained, pressing his eyes shut and pinching the bridge of his nose. "My sister blew through her monthly allowance again, and she needs a loan to tide her over until the end of the month."

"Her monthly allowance? Is she a college student?"

Amusement filled his eyes. "No, higher learning isn't exactly her thing."

"What does she do for a living?" Sharleen asked.

"You mean besides shopping at Lenox Square?"

Emilio finished his wine, then settled back in the booth. He looked calm, as relaxed as a sunbather on the beach, but she sensed his unease. "Did your sister move with you to Atlanta?"

"Francesca got pregnant shortly after she graduated from high school, and to avoid a scandal in my hometown, my father sent her here to live with me," he explained. "At the time she was an aspiring model working with several Italian fashion houses, but she put her career on hold to raise Lucca."

"How did you feel about your father's decision?"

"I thought it was great, and when my nephew was born, it brought us even closer together."

"Having a baby in the house must have cramped your style."

"No, not at all. I adored Lucca, and I raised him as my own." Emilio sighed deeply. "It's been two years since he passed away, but I still can't believe he's gone."

Sharleen moved closer and rested a hand on his shoulder.

"My whole world fell apart when Lucca died." His voice broke, and he dropped his gaze to his lap. "I stayed in bed for weeks after his funeral and struggled with insomnia for months."

"That must have been an incredibly difficult time for you."

"It still is."

"It doesn't have to be. You can put the past behind you and enjoy a rich, fulfilling life."

A pained expression darkened his face. "I don't deserve to be happy," he said coolly. "I messed up, and because of my selfishness and stupidity, my nephew's gone forever."

"Do you want to talk about what happened?"

He shook his head. "I can't."

"Then let it go." Sharleen held his gaze, didn't back down when anger blazed like fire in the depths of his eyes. "Instead of punishing yourself for something you can't change, do something to honor your nephew's memory."

Surprise flickered across his face, and he stared at her for a long, tense moment.

"Start a charity foundation in his name, establish a scholarship program for low-income students or share your personal story with a parent support group," she continued. "Speaking publicly about your loss will be a cathartic, worthwhile experience that could help change lives."

Emilio raised an eyebrow. "I thought you weren't going to boss me around or cram your opinions down my throat?"

"I'm not. I'm simply making a few helpful suggestions. The decision is ultimately yours."

"I like your suggestions."

And I like how you make me feel.

Relaxing on the patio, talking with Emilio, Sharleen marveled at how open and honest he was. He was making progress, slowly coming out of his shell, and she was thrilled about it. As the night wore on, he revealed more details about himself. Things Sharleen was shocked to discover. He'd been bullied as a child, felt enormous pressure to live up to his father's expectations, and despite his illustrious racing career, he struggled with self-doubt. "Are you close to your other siblings or just Francesca?" she asked.

"My older brother and I used to be tight, but we haven't spoken in years."

"Why? What happened?"

Emilio tugged at his collar, avoided her gaze. "I can't tell you. You'll think I'm a pig."

"I'm not here to pass judgment. I'm here to support you and help you grow."

"I like that."

And I like you. Sharleen caught herself before the words left her mouth.

"I accidentally slept with his fiancée."

"How?" she asked, stunned. "You didn't know they were engaged?"

"No, but Immanuel's convinced I seduced her."

"Did you?"

"Family means everything to me, and I'd never do anything to dishonor someone I love."

Sharleen believed him, sensed he was telling her the truth. Emilio had nothing to gain by lying to her, and he didn't strike her as the kind of guy who'd betray his flesh and blood. "Have you tried reaching out to him?"

"Yes, but with no luck. Immanuel hates my guts, and I don't blame him. I was a jerk during my racing days and thought the world revolved around me."

She widened her eyes and cupped her cheeks with her hands. "A superstar athlete with a massive ego? No, no, say it ain't so!"

Emilio laughed, and the sound of his hearty chuckle made her body warm all over.

"Enough about my dysfunctional family. Let's talk about you."

Caught off guard, she struggled to speak. "What do you, um, want to know?"

"What do you do on the weekends?"

"On Saturdays I work from home, and on Sundays I volunteer at The Salvation Army."

"How long have you been volunteering there?"

"Since birth," she said, with a laugh. "My mother was the director of Outreach Services, so I had no choice. When I wasn't helping my dad at his shop, I was at the center, lending a hand."

"You're fulfilling her life's work."

"I prefer to think of it as doing my part. Did you know forty-six million Americans live in poverty?"

"No, I'm embarrassed to say I didn't. Maybe one day I'll volunteer, too."

"Why put off tomorrow what you can do today?" Sharleen glanced at her wristwatch. "If we hurry, we can make it to the center in time to serve dinner. They're always short of volunteers, and they could use a strong, strapping fella like you in the kitchen."

"You're serious?"

"Absolutely." She grabbed her purse and slid out of the booth. "Are you coming?"

"How can I refuse when you asked so nicely?" he teased, his eyes alight with mischief. Emilio took his keys out of his pocket and rose to his feet. "Let's go."

"Oh, wait, we haven't paid the bill."

"It's cool. I have a running tab." He winked and pulled her close to his side. "My cousin Nicco owns the Dolce Vita franchise. He knows I'm good for it."

Sharleen sighed in relief. "Thank God. I thought you were pulling a dine and dash!"

As they stood at the restaurant entrance, waiting for the valet to return with Emilio's car, he told her more about growing up in Italy, his troubled teenage years and his first amateur race. He spoke with great passion about his career, and Sharleen couldn't help but wonder if he exhibited the same level of excitement in the bedroom.

There's only one way to find out, whispered her inner voice. *Tell Emilio you're attracted to him, and let the chips fall where they may.*

Sharleen chased away the thought, booted it out of her mind. Not because she didn't desire him—she did, more than she'd ever desired anyone—but deep down, she knew that Emilio Morretti would never be interested in someone like her.

Chapter 8

"Got a minute for your favorite client?"

Antwan glanced up from the document he was reading and dropped his Montblanc pen on his desk. "Emilio? Is that you?" Rising to his feet, he rubbed his eyes as if he couldn't believe what he was seeing and gave his head a hard shake. "My eyes must be playing tricks on me, because you haven't been to my office in years!"

Indulging in a hearty chuckle, Emilio glanced around the lavish surroundings. Proud of his accomplishments and wealth, Antwan had decorated his office with the best furniture, artwork and electronics money could buy. Electric blue walls and Oriental rugs gave the room a luxurious feel, and a glass shelf held more baseball memorabilia than a sports museum.

"It's great to see you, man." Dressed in a three-button

suit and burgundy tie, Antwan strode confidently around
his desk and clapped Emilio on the back. "I haven't seen
you look this good in years…"

I know, and Sharleen's the reason why.

"I was planning to come to Greensboro this afternoon to speak to you."

"You were? Why? What's up?"

"I'll share my good news in a minute, but first I want
to know what's up with you," he said, leaning against
the front of his desk. "The last time we spoke you were
bummed out and depressed."

"I miss Lucca, and it hurts like hell that he's gone,
but I'm in a good place right now." At night, in moments of despair, when he relived his nephew's accident, he didn't reach for a bottle of scotch. During
those dark, depressing moments he thought about Sharleen. She'd lost both of her parents as a teenager, but
she still maintained a positive outlook on life. She in-
spired him, encouraged him and cheered him up when
he was down. He admired her keen mind *and* the sexy,
curvy package it came in. He'd fallen hard for her and
often imagined their lives together as a couple. It was
a shocking thought, considering he'd never had a successful relationship, but he wanted her to be his girl,
and he wasn't afraid to admit it. Problem was, every
time he tried to talk to her about his feelings, she
swiftly changed the subject.

"How are things going with Sharleen?" Antwan adjusted his suit jacket and crossed his legs at the ankles.
"Are you guys butting heads or getting along swim-
mingly?"

A proud grin claimed Emilio's mouth. He felt as if
he'd known Sharleen all of his life, and he still couldn't

believe they'd met only three weeks earlier. He was comfortable with her, completely at ease in her presence, and looked forward to seeing her every day. During their coaching sessions, they exercised in his home gym, whipped up healthy meals in his kitchen or hung out in his media room, talking and playing pool. Emilio enjoyed her fun-loving personality, her optimistic nature and their poignant discussions about life. He found it refreshing to be with someone who'd rather discuss social issues than Justin Bieber's latest run-in with the law.

He thought back to their coaching session last Friday and smiled as their flirtatious exchange played in his mind. Despite being only twenty-seven years old, Sharleen always looked so prim and proper, as if she were going to lunch with the First Lady. When she'd arrived at his estate in one of her trademark outfits, he couldn't resist teasing her.

"Do you ever wear anything besides cardigans and dress pants?" he'd asked.

"You wouldn't take me seriously if I dressed like a pinup girl."

"That's true," he'd conceded. "But seeing you in a pair of Daisy Dukes would *definitely* make for a more interesting session."

"Keep dreaming!" she'd said, her tone full of attitude and sass. "Now, go get your life plan, or I'll tell your golf buddies you tear up watching chick flicks!"

Her joke still made him laugh. Emilio couldn't believe how much his life had changed since meeting Sharleen, how rejuvenated he felt. She asked him tough questions and didn't let up until he answered them openly and honestly. These days, he wasn't cooped up in the house watching old home videos; he was busier than ever. He volunteered at The Salvation Army three days a week, played coed soccer at the YMCA and attended support-group meetings at Pathways Center on Wednesday nights. Thankfully, no one at the center recognized him, and to his surprise, at the end of every session he felt less stressed-out and more hopeful about his future. The dark cloud that had been hanging over his head since Lucca's death had finally lifted, and Sharleen Nichols was the reason why.

"We're getting along great." Emilio didn't want Antwan to know he was interested in Sharleen romantically, so he wiped the lopsided grin off of his face. "I hate to admit it, but you were right. She's smart, insightful and tough as nails. Sharleen doesn't let me get away with anything, and when I complain, she gives me an earful!"

Antwan wore a proud smile. "That's my girl."

No, she's my *girl.* Yesterday, during their afternoon coaching session, he'd spoken openly about his tumultuous childhood, his strained relationship with his father and the pressures of fame. Sharleen told him what he needed to hear—not what he wanted to hear—and encouraged him to focus on the future, not the mistakes of his past. And when he walked her back to her car hours later, Emilio realized he didn't want her to leave—cvcr.

"I'm glad you guys hit it off. I was worried you'd give her a hard time and she'd quit."

"I'd never do that," Emilio shot back, disappointed that his manager thought so little of him. "I know a good woman when I see one, and Sharleen Nichols is the real deal."

The desk phone buzzed, but Antwan didn't move.

"Well, I'll be damned." Cocking his head to the right, he stroked the length of his jaw. "You're sweet on her, aren't you?"

Pretending he didn't hear the question, Emilio picked up a baseball off the glass shelf and admired his cousin's signature. He'd given the autographed ball to Antwan for Christmas years earlier and grinned when he remembered how his business manager had jumped for joy when he opened the gift box. His cousin Demetri Morretti was not only a talented baseball player, but also a class act. Emilio respected him, and although they didn't speak often, he valued his opinion. *I need to get in touch with Demetri, Nicco and Rafael. I miss those guys, and I want them to meet Sharleen the next time they're in town.*

"Does Sharleen know how you feel? Have you told her?" Antwan pressed. "Is she interested in you, too?"

Emilio wriggled his eyebrows, as if he were amused, but he knew his business manager could see through his flimsy charade. Antwan had always been able to read him like a book. "There's nothing going on between us."

"Not yet, but it's just a matter of time."

I sure hope so, because I'm tired of being a gentleman. I want to kiss her, and love her, and—

"I don't know why I'm surprised," Antwan continued. "This is nothing new. All of Sharleen's male clients end up falling in love with her."

Emilio felt his eyes fly out of his head. "They do?"

"Of course. What's not to love? She's a strong, intelligent woman with a great head on her shoulders, and men naturally gravitate toward her." He gave a dismissive shrug. "You're not the first client to fall for her, and you won't be the last."

Oh, yes, I will. You just wait and see!

"Sharleen's a hot commodity on the Atlanta social scene, and several guys are pursuing her right now."

His mind reeling, Emilio took a moment to catch his breath. His heart was beating so fast he feared it would conk out. His lips felt like sandpaper, coarse and dry, but he asked the question on the tip of his tongue. "Are you sure?"

"We have a lot of the same friends, and her love life is a popular topic. Apparently, she gets around."

Emilio dropped down onto the leather chair in front of Antwan's desk. He couldn't stomach the thought of Sharleen being with another man, didn't want to believe she was like all of the other promiscuous women who threw themselves at him. But his gut feeling was that his friend was telling him the truth. The realization that Sharleen wasn't the woman he *thought* she was made his heart ache.

Why should her past matter? You haven't exactly been a Boy Scout.

"Don't get me wrong." Antwan picked up his oversize coffee mug and took a swig. "I love Sharleen, and I think she's a fantastic woman, but I could never date someone with more lovers than me. Call me sexist, but that's just how I feel."

"Then you won't mind if I ask her out."

Antwan's face tensed, hardened into a dark, angry mask, but he spoke in a jovial tone. "Why would I? It's a free world. You can date whoever you want."

"I know, but I don't want there to be any bad blood between us."

Antwan scoffed. "Bad blood over a piece of ass? Man, please, I'm bigger than that."

"This isn't about sex."

"Yes, it is. With you, it's *always* about sex."

"Not this time," Emilio insisted. "Sharleen has been incredible the last few weeks, and I think she's special."

"Hooking up with her is nothing but a game to you. It's all about the thrill of the chase, the adrenaline rush, and once you hit it you'll be on to the next girl."

Images of making love to Sharleen bombarded his mind. His heartbeat sped up, pounded in his ears, and an erection grew inside his pants. He was attracted to her, sure, but he wanted more than just a sexual relationship. They had a strong connection, a tight bond, and he suspected she was interested in him, too. The thought heartened him, made his chest puff up with pride. It wasn't anything she'd said; it was the way she looked at him, how her eyes lit up when he "accidentally" touched her. Yesterday, after she'd left his estate, he'd sat down and planned the perfect date for her, and he was anxious to put his plan into action.

Emilio heard his cell phone buzz and knew his latest text message was from Francesca. He pulled out his phone.

We need to talk. I'll drop by the house once I finish at the beauty salon.

Feeling heaviness in his chest, he wondered how much money his kid sister wanted this time. Every week she needed something—a flashier, more expensive car, spending money for a girls-only trip to Paris, to-die-for diamond earrings from Cartier—and her constant financial demands were weighing him down.

The problem was he couldn't say no to her. Not after what had happened to Lucca.

During one of their recent coaching sessions, Sharleen had said he was setting up Francesca to fail in the real word, and she'd encouraged him to cut the purse strings. But Emilio didn't know if he could do it. He wanted his sister to be happy and didn't want to do anything to ruin their relationship. He'd lost Immanuel, and he didn't want to lose Francesca, too.

"Since you're here, I might as well bring you up to speed about my video conference with Ferrari this morning." Straightening to his full height, Antwan slid his hands into the pockets of his dress pants and smiled broadly. "They miss you, and they're willing to pay seven figures to get you back behind the wheel of one of their race cars…"

Leaning back in his chair, Emilio suppressed a deep sigh. He didn't want to talk about his career—he wanted to talk about Sharleen. Dozens of questions filled his mind, and the more he considered what Antwan had said the more confused he was. Was she serious about any of her other suitors? Was their "connection" just wishful thinking on his part?

"And that's not all. Ferrari wants you to be their new spokesperson."

Emilio surfaced from his thoughts. "I'll think about it."

"Don't bother. They needed an answer right away, so I accepted on your behalf."

"I didn't agree to that."

"It was the smart thing to do," Antwan said tightly.

"For who? Me or your bank account?"

Antwan's eyes narrowed, and his nostrils flared.

"The next time you pull a stunt like that, you're fired." Emilio clenched his teeth. "It's my career, not yours. I do what I want, not what you tell me to do. Got it?"

The men stared each other down.

"I know you miss Lucca, but it's time to move on. You've mourned him long enough." Antwan wore a sympathetic face, but there was a bitter edge to his voice. "Ferrari is rolling out the red carpet for you, and if you thumb your nose at them, they'll never work with you again."

"You should have talked to me first, before you accepted the offer."

"You're right," he conceded. "I'm sorry. I wasn't thinking. It won't happen again."

Despite himself, Emilio chuckled. "Right. Now say that with a straight face!"

Emilio listened as Antwan outlined the specifics of the deal and made a mental note to discuss it with Sharleen. He wanted her input and wondered how she'd feel about him traveling around the world for industry events. "When will the contracts be ready?"

"In a few weeks, but as a show of good faith I think you should attend the Miami Exotic Car Show on Memorial Day weekend. Executives from Ferrari will be at the event, and they'd be stoked to see you signing autographs, posing for pictures and kissing babies."

"Antwan, I'm a race-car driver, not a politician."

His manager gave a hearty laugh. "Just make sure you're in Miami for the event."

"Maybe I'll invite Sharleen to come," he said, thinking out loud.

"Don't bother. She hates the Magic City. Said the heat gets to her."

Then I'll just have to change her mind. Emilio liked the idea of having fun in the sun with Sharleen and decided he'd call his cousin Nicco once he got back to his car. The acclaimed restaurateur was a regular fixture on the Miami night scene, and he knew the best places to party. He'd ask his cousin to use his connections to score concert tickets, movie-premiere passes and reservations at the best restaurants in town. *I'm going to go all out to impress her,* he decided. *And by the end of the weekend Sharleen's going to be my lady...*

"Let's discuss how to invest your signing bonus." Antwan sat down behind his desk and grabbed his Montblanc pen. "Do you have any ideas?"

"Pay off the tax bill, donate a million dollars to The Salvation Army and deposit the rest in my savings account."

The pen fell from Antwan's hand.

Anticipating his reaction, Emilio waited for the moment to pass. Emilio felt as if he'd been given a second chance, a new lease on life, and this time around he wanted to use his wealth for good.

"You're punking me, right?" Antwan said, with a nervous laugh.

"It's my money, and I can spend it any way I see fit."

"A million-dollar donation is outrageous. Give them a hundred grand. That's enough."

"I wasn't asking your permission."

Curses fell from Antwan's mouth, and the muscles in his neck pulsed and twitched. "As your business manager, it's my job to stop you from blowing your winnings. But if you continue to disregard my advice and keep spending lavishly, there's nothing I can do."

"Spending lavishly?" Emilio repeated, baffled by his words. "I'm not buying a private island off the coast of Belize. I'm giving money to a worthy cause, and if you don't like it, that's too bad."

"Fine," he grumbled. "Do what you want, but don't say I didn't warn you."

As casual as he could, he asked the question that had been circling his mind for weeks, the one he'd spoken to Sharleen about at length last night.

"When is the qualifying race for the World Series Racing All-Star Race? Is it too late to enter?"

Antwan's eyebrows rose.

"I think the race will be fun, and I'd love to work with my old pit crew again."

Antwan pumped his fists in the air. "Yes! Finally! I *knew* Sharleen could do it!"

Emilio frowned. "You knew she could do what?"

"Help you rediscover your purpose in life, of course." His eyes were filled with enthusiasm, and he was so excited he was rocking eagerly in his chair. "Being a race-car driver is in your DNA, what you were born to do, and you'll never be fulfilled doing anything else."

To Emilio's surprise, he agreed with the statement, knew in his heart that it was true.

"I can't wait to share the good news on Twitter. Your fans are going to go wild."

"You're getting way ahead of yourself." Emilio stood. "I never said I was coming out of retirement, so don't post anything online. I'll compete in the All-Star Race, and if I place in the top three, I'll evaluate my options."

"You'll win. You always do. Hell, they should just give you the trophy now!"

The men chuckled, then spent the next few minutes discussing the All-Star Race.

"Get in touch with your old pit crew," Antwan advised. "You haven't been to the track in years, and it's going to take a while for you to get your skills back, so the more practice the better."

"Thanks, Dad," Emilio joked, pulling his car keys out of his back pocket.

"Where are you going? I haven't told you about negotiations with Nike—"

"Another time. I'm meeting Sharleen at three thirty, and I don't want to be late."

Antwan's face fell, but he quickly recovered and nodded his head.

"Let me know when the contracts are in. We can review them together."

"I will. Give my regards to Sharleen," he said quietly. "Have fun."

You can count on it, Emilio thought, slipping on his sunglasses as he exited the office. *I'm spending the afternoon with a vibrant, vivacious woman, and one day soon she'll be my girlfriend.*

Chapter 9

The sleek black helicopter climbed high above the trees and headed toward Atlanta. Sharleen wondered which one of Emilio's obscenely rich neighbors owned the gleaming chopper. Uncomfortable in confined spaces, she couldn't imagine ever being inside such a small aircraft, but suspected the view from above was breathtaking. *Probably,* her inner voice conceded. *But nothing beats spending the afternoon with Emilio.*

Sharleen jogged beside Emilio on the winding trail, awed by the beauty around her. The air was perfumed with the scent of plants, exotic flowers and sweet-smelling herbs.

Pressing her eyes shut, she inhaled the fresh air. A sense of calm washed over her, instantly relaxed her. She loved feeling the sun on her face and the wind in her hair. But what she enjoyed most about being in Greensboro was hanging out with her favorite client.

Emilio is more than just a client. You like him more than you've ever liked anyone, and if he kissed you, you'd probably die of pleasure!

Stealing a glance at him, she felt her heart murmur inside her chest. Athletes had always been her weakness, and the tall, wickedly handsome race-car driver was everything she wanted in a man. The realization stunned her, but deep down in her heart she knew it was true. Her gaze slid down his physique. His fitted white T-shirt and black athletic shorts showcased a flat stomach, toned biceps and muscled legs. But it was his smoldering gaze that made her head spin time and time again. He had his nephew's face tattooed on his left biceps, and the adorable image made her smile. It took supreme effort, but she peeled her eyes away from his chiseled body and asked about his morning meeting. "How did it go? Did you make a decision about the All-Star Race?"

Emilio told her about his argument with Antwan, his new blockbuster deal with Ferrari and his hour-long conversation with his pit crew. "We're practicing tomorrow at the Atlanta Motor Speedway, and I want you to be there. You're my good-luck charm, and my crew is anxious to meet you."

"They are? Why? What did you tell them?"

"Nothing just that I'd met the girl of my dreams."

Sharleen gave a shaky laugh. She couldn't tell if Emilio was serious or pulling her leg, but convinced herself it was the latter. Normally, she ignored clients who flirted with her, but that strategy wasn't working with Emilio. If anything, his teasing made her desire him even more.

"I need you to be at my first practice."

His words surprised her, made her realize how much he'd changed in the past three weeks. Instead of moping around the house, he was attending social events, volunteering at outreach programs and making plans for the future. He was even actively looking for ways to honor his nephew's memory. Sharleen had encouraged him to attend meetings at the clinic, and to her surprise, he was always the first one to arrive. He didn't talk during group sessions, but he admitted that hearing other people's stories made him feel less lonely. These days, Emilio was fun to be around, and everyone from his publicist to his physical trainer was thrilled about the positive changes he'd made in his life.

"Are you listening or fantasizing about me again?" he teased. "Don't try and deny it, because I can see the truth in your pretty brown eyes."

Sharleen parted her lips to speak and tripped over her tongue. She was mortified that she'd lost her composure again and inwardly chastised herself for letting her nerves get the best of her.

Emilio had a hold on her she just couldn't explain, and the more she fought their attraction the stronger it was. It was times like this, when he was flirting with her, that she remembered he was one of the most eligible bachelors in the nation. Unlike the guys she'd casually dated in the past, he made her feel special and seemed to get a kick out of spoiling her. He had flowers delivered to her office, treated her to lunch at trendy eateries and lavished her with time and attention. It was hard not to think wanton thoughts when he flashed his trademark grin at her, but Sharleen was determined to keep her cool. Her reputation and the vice-president position were at stake, and she'd worked too damned hard to watch her career go up in smoke. And she had to land the VP position so she could persuade her boss to fire Brad and rehire Jocelyn. Her best friend still hadn't found a job, and she was growing more discouraged each day.

"I'll pick you up at nine o'clock, so we can drive down together."

"Emilio, I can't. I'm going with a client to Raleigh tomorrow and I won't be back until Thursday."

"What's in North Carolina?"

"My client is attending a funeral and wanted me there for emotional support."

He narrowed his eyes. "Is your client male or female?"

"Female. Why?"

"Just checking," he said, with a wink. "Do you routinely travel with clients?"

"Sometimes. It depends on the situation."

"I'm glad to hear that, because I'm going to Miami over Memorial Day weekend, and I want you to come. Antwan wants me to attend the Exotic Car Show—"

"It's not about what Antwan wants. It's about what *you* want."

"I'm psyched about going to Miami, but…" He broke off speaking and expelled a deep breath. "I haven't been to any public events since Lucca died, and even though I'm excited about reconnecting with my fans, I'm nervous, too."

"That's understandable, but try not to worry. Your fans adore you, *especially* the female ones, and I'm sure they'll welcome you back with open arms."

"I can't go without you, Sharleen. I need you by my side…"

His words sounded poetic, like the lyrics to a love song, and his dreamy accent made her feel light-headed. That was why going out of town with him was out of the question. There was no telling what would happen in Miami, and she didn't want to lose her job *or* her heart to him. Not wanting to hurt his feelings, she said, "I'll check my schedule, and I'll get back to you in a few days."

"Why don't you save yourself the time and trouble and say yes now?"

Because I hate hot weather, scantily dressed women flaunting their perfect bodies and pool parties. I never know what to wear, and I don't want to feel self-conscious about my—

"Do you want me to call your boss and ask her permission?"

"That's not…um…"

Emilio lifted the bottom of his shirt, exposing his abs, and wiped the sweat from his face. Sharleen's brain turned to mush. Seeing his bare chest caused her body to tingle and quiver. Her sexual urges were powerful, unlike anything she'd experienced. Staring at him, she envisioned them kissing, could almost taste and feel his mouth against hers.

"I'll call Mrs. Fontaine tomorrow and square things with her."

Sharleen snapped out of her thoughts. "No, please don't. That won't be necessary."

"Great, then I'll have my assistant finalize our travel arrangements." His smile returned, blazed so bright it made the sun look dull. "You'll have your own room at my cottage at Fisher Island resort and plenty of time to shop at the malls and boutiques."

"Are you spending the entire weekend at the car show?"

Emilio shook his head. "No. I'll be busy romancing you."

Sharleen swallowed hard, told herself he was just teasing her. She considered her options, thoroughly weighed the pros and cons of going out of town with Emilio. Mrs. Fontaine was going to make a decision about the VP position at the end of the month, and she didn't want to ruin her chances of landing the job by upsetting her boss. It was better not to rock the boat. "Sometimes you can be *so* difficult," she teased, rolling her eyes in an exaggerated fashion. "Do you always have to get your way?"

"Yes, Ms. Nichols, as a matter of fact, I do."

He leaned into her, got so close their arms were touching.

"Do you know what I want right now?" His gaze dropped to her mouth, and he licked his lips with deliberate slowness, as if his sole purpose in life was to arouse her with his tongue. "She's tall and curvy and smells like jasmine."

Desire surged through her veins, made her heart hammer inside her chest. Afraid she'd fall victim to lust, she turned to admire the lily pond, instead of Emilio's juicy lips. "This is an amazing view," she said. "Do you jog down here often?"

"No, but now that I have you to keep me company I'll be getting out a lot more."

"No way, José! Count me out. This is the last time I let you talk me into going for a jog," she said. "I'm so tired I could lie down on the grass and fall asleep!"

Emilio cracked up. "Don't be so hard on yourself.

You're doing great." He looked her over, took his time appraising her. "And you look gorgeous, too."

"Right," she drawled, swatting at the pesky flies buzzing around her. "Sweat is *real* sexy."

"Not sweat, per se, but you certainly are."

A girlish grin exploded onto her lips, a smile so wide it made her jaw ache. "I thought Stiletto Aerobics was hard, but it's a piece of cake compared to this."

"Stiletto Aerobics? Sounds erotic. How about a demonstration after lunch?"

To her surprise, his words excited her, turned her on. Her breasts ached for his touch, her nipples hardened under her long-sleeve shirt and a delicious shudder ripped through her body. Sharleen wanted to pounce on him, to kiss him shamelessly, and it took every ounce of her self-control not to devour him. "Emilio, you don't have to cook for me every time I come over."

"Yes, I do. The quickest way to a woman's heart is through her stomach, and I'm hoping you'll profess your undying love after you taste my lobster risotto."

"My, my, aren't we ambitious."

"Well, I *did* win three World Series Racing championships."

"Relationships aren't a competitive sport."

"Tell that to my ex-girlfriend." His smile disappeared. "She loved playing mind games, and I never knew where I stood with her..."

I'd never treat you like that, Sharleen thought, gazing at his handsome profile. *If you were my man I'd be open and honest, and I'd tell you I love you every single day.*

"Most of the women I hooked up with in the past were more interested in the glamorous lifestyle than me, but I was too busy blowing through my earnings to care," he confessed. "But at this point in my life, I'm ready to have a family and kids, and I won't settle for less."

I'd love to have your babies. The thought shocked Sharleen, and for the second time in minutes, goose bumps pricked her skin.

They jogged through the neighborhood, along the lake and past the park. Jokes flew, laughter abounded and their conversation flowed smoothly from one topic to the next. Sharleen coached other celebrities, but no one made her laugh like Emilio. He had great stories, and his dry wit made her crack up time and time again. She'd probably never go zip-lining in Costa Rica, or paragliding in Tanzania, but she enjoyed hearing about his adventures abroad. Two hours passed, but she was having so much fun with Emilio that she didn't want to go home. "Where do you go when you want to get away from everything?" she asked. "Venice? Sydney? Maui?"

"No, Monte Carlo. Have you ever been?"

Sharleen shook her head. "No, never, but I'd love to visit there one day."

"When you're ready to make the trip, we'll fly there in the Morretti private jet."

"What's so special about Monte Carlo?"

"They call it the playground of the rich, but there's more to the city than just fast cars, fine dining and million-dollar yachts. I love the museums, the striking architecture and the extreme sports, of course."

"You won your first World Series Racing championship in Monte Carlo."

Emilio wore a sheepish smile. "You read my bio."

"A good life coach always does."

The estate came into view, and Sharleen sighed in relief.

"Do you want to take a break, or would you like to keep going?"

"No way. I'm exhausted, and my legs are killing me. I may pass out right here!"

He stopped abruptly. His gaze was full of longing, and his mouth was just inches away from her face. "What can I do to help?"

You mean besides kissing me passionately?

The air around them was electrified, charged with sexual tension. Sharleen had never had such strong feelings for someone and wondered how much longer she could fight their attraction. These days, Emilio was all she could think of. It didn't matter if she was job hunting with Jocelyn or puttering around in her garden— thoughts of him overwhelmed her mind. Emilio proved that nice guys still existed, that all men weren't dogs, and she loved being with him.

"I'd do anything for you. You know that, right?" Emilio said.

He reached out and brushed his fingers ever so gently against her cheeks. Pleasure shot straight to her core, tickled and teased her flesh.

"Do you want me to carry you back to my estate?"

"Let's not and say we did," she said with a laugh. "In case you haven't noticed, I'm a curvy woman, *not* a toothpick, and I don't want you to hurt yourself."

His stare was bold, penetrating. Emilio didn't speak, didn't utter a word, but if looks could kill she'd be six feet under. Sharleen gulped. *What did I do wrong? Why is he mad at me?*

The tense moment lasted for only a few seconds, but it felt as if hours had passed.

Emilio broke the silence, and his voice was hollow, cold as ice. He didn't yell at her, but his disappointment was evident. "You're an incredibly smart woman, but I swear, sometimes you say the craziest things."

Sharleen narrowed her eyes and hitched a hand to her hip. "Who are you calling crazy?"

"You. Now shut up and kiss me." Emilio seized her waist, wrapped his arms around her and claimed her lips with his mouth.

Chapter 10

The moment Emilio's lips touched Sharleen's mouth, pleasure exploded inside of her body. He tasted of peppermint—delicious and sweet—and the savory flavor tickled her taste buds. Tingles danced down her spine as he sprayed soft, featherlight kisses over her lips and cheeks. *Is this* really *happening? Are we actually kissing, or is this a figment of my imagination?*

Emilio pulled her closer, urged her into his arms. His hands explored her flesh, caressed and stroked her inflamed body. He played with her hair, massaged her neck, her shoulders and hips. Sharleen was stunned by how aggressive he was, but she secretly loved every minute of it. For the first time in her life, she was living in the moment, gratifying the desires of her flesh, and it was the most liberating thing she'd ever done.

Delirious with need, she inclined her head toward

him and deepened the kiss. He wasn't a good kisser—
he was an outstanding kisser, the best she'd ever had.
Sharleen wanted more of him, needed more. She didn't
want the kiss to ever end, could happily spend the rest
of the day cradled in his arms. His urgent caress and
the warmth of his touch intensified her hunger, and as
the seconds slipped into minutes, Sharleen found herself losing control. Her temperature soared, and the
voices in her head—the ones urging her to flee—faded
to the background.

Sharleen stroked his face, grabbed fistfuls of his
hair, nibbled his bottom lip. The heady sensation of
his lips and his hands was overwhelming, pushed her
to the brink. Overcome with longing, a hunger she'd
never known, she moaned from deep inside. Finally,
after weeks of flirting, they'd kissed, and it was even
better than she'd imagined.

Their moans and groans intensified, grew to a fe-
vered pitch. Desperate to be closer to him, she draped
her hands around his neck and pressed her body flat
against his. It wasn't enough—she needed more, desired more. A shiver ripped through her body, one so
powerful her knees buckled.

Sharleen couldn't believe that one kiss—one sensuous, erotic kiss—could wreak such havoc inside of
her body, but it did. Her breasts ached for his touch,
her hands shook and her legs quivered. She wanted
to rip off his clothes and kiss every inch of his body.
The thought made her cheeks burn with shame, but the
urge still remained.

Finally, they pulled apart, exhausted.

"That was some kiss," Emilio said in a husky growl.
"Definitely the best I've ever had."

Not trusting herself to speak, Sharleen took a moment to catch her breath. She lifted her head, caught his eye and returned his smile. She couldn't deny how much she'd enjoyed that kiss, and she tried to keep thoughts of losing her job from ruining the moment.

"I'm sorry I lost control, but I couldn't help myself. Your lips are so damn tempting."

"I know," she said, with a shrug, pretending to inspect her French manicure. "I hear that *all* the time."

Emilio chuckled. "I love your humility. It's endearing."

"At least I'm not rude." Deciding to have some fun with him, she jabbed a finger at his chest and wore a stern face. "Make no mistake, Mr. Morretti. The next time you tell me to 'shut up,' you'll be looking for a new life coach."

"That suits me just fine."

Her spirits sank. "I thought you liked working with me."

"I do, but I don't want you to be my life coach anymore. I want you to be my girlfriend."

Sharleen heard a gasp fall out of her mouth.

"Why is it so hard for you to believe that I'm attracted to you and that I want us to date?"

Because you've dated models and actresses, and I'm a nobody. Her thoughts spun out of control. She knew it would be foolish to embark on a relationship with him—the risk of being hurt was just too great.

"I adore everything about you. You're intelligent, ridiculously beautiful and—"

"Ridiculously beautiful?" Sharleen scoffed and rolled her eyes. Men would say anything to get laid, and although she'd never pegged Emilio as the type who'd use lies and flattery to lure her into bed, he seemed to be doing just that. "Laying it on kinda thick, aren't you?"

"No. I think you're perfect." His gaze was a lethal combination of hunger and desire. It held her captive, refused to let her go. "You have great eyes, pretty lips and bootylicious curves!"

Sharleen cracked up, chuckled until tears filled her eyes. The word *bootylicious* had no business coming out of Emilio's Italian mouth, and the expression on his face tugged at her heartstrings. He made her laugh, even at his own expense. He was the most caring man she'd ever met. *It's too bad he's my client. If he wasn't I'd definitely want him to be my—*

"Are you free on Saturday night? I'd like to take you out for dinner. On a date."

"I don't know what to say."

"Say, 'I'd love to. I'll be ready at six.'"

"I can't," she said, smiling apologetically. "Dating clients is against the rules, and if Mrs. Fontaine finds out we're seeing each other, she'll fire me."

"You don't need to work. I'll take care of you."

"Emilio, I can take care of myself, and that's beside the point. I love working at Pathways, and I'd be devastated if I lost my job. Being a life coach is all I've ever wanted to do."

"I understand, and for now, I'll respect your wishes. On Saturday we'll have dinner here at the house, then watch the new Will Smith movie in my theater."

Sharleen heaved a deep breath and tried to gather her bearings, but the truth came tumbling out of her mouth. "Dating is a bad idea. We would never work. We're from two different worlds—"

"I don't care. I want you, and *only* you."

"Why?" she blurted out, stunned by his confession. "You can have any woman you want, so why are you pursuing me?"

"Because you have no ulterior motives. I can be myself around you, without fear of you selling me out to the tabloids or betraying my trust." Emilio leaned in, gave her a sweet, soft kiss on the lips, then nuzzled his face against her cheek. "And you smell great, too."

A grin tickled her lips. "I do, huh?"

"I love your fragrance. It reminds me of my villa in Lake Como. One day I'll take you there, and we'll make love in the garden."

Oh, my, she thought, fanning a hand to her face. *Let's leave tonight!*

Emilio entwined his fingers with hers and led her across the backyard toward the house. The backyard had it all: an outdoor kitchen, whirlpool tubs surrounded by lush plants and shrubs, waterproof flat-screen TVs and a decorative fire pit. As they strode past the car-shaped swimming pool, Sharleen decided the estate was as lavish as a five-star resort.

"Do you know how to swim?" Emilio asked.

"Yes, but I rarely go swimming."

"Why not?"

"I haven't found the right bathing suit," she joked, returning his smile. "Besides, it's just not my thing."

"I'm going to buy you some designer swimwear. We're going to spend the day at Miami Beach with my cousin and his wife, and I want to see you in a string bikini."

Sharleen gulped. *I can't wear a bikini. People will point and stare!*

"We can discuss our trip to Miami during lunch." Emilio slipped a hand around her waist and held her tight. "Since the weather's nice, I thought we could eat outside."

A savory aroma carried on the breeze, tickling her nose and rousing her hunger. Her gaze landed on the gazebo. The table was dressed with red table linens, fine china that gleamed and sparkled and two bottles of Cristal champagne. An oversize bouquet sat beside the potted candles, and lace ribbon was swathed around the chairs. "Wow, what an elaborate spread. What's the occasion?"

A grin claimed his lips. "We met a month ago today."

"And you think that's worth celebrating?"

"Absolutely." He pulled out her chair and stepped aside. "Meeting you was the best thing that's ever happened to me, and I hope today is the first of many celebrations."

At a loss for words, Sharleen sat down and dropped her hands in her lap. Everything was happening too fast, at lightning-quick speed. Her apprehension must have shown on her face, because Emilio crouched down in front of her and slowly stroked her cheek with his fingertips. "I don't want anyone else. I want you today, tomorrow and for the rest of my life."

"Emilio, this is crazy. We've only known each other for a month—"

"The moment I saw you, I knew you were the only woman for me."

"Was that before or after you kicked me out of your estate?"

His eyes dimmed, and the smile slid off of his face.

"That was a tough day for me," he confessed, his

voice filled with sadness. "It was the second anniversary of Lucca's death, and I was angry at the world."

"I know, and I'm not trying to be insensitive. All I'm saying is—"

"You're making excuses for why we can't be together, but I won't let you push me away. My feelings for you are real, and I won't give up on us."

They are? Really? You're not just saying that because you want to get me into bed? Sharleen kept her thoughts to herself, didn't speak. His words played in her mind over and over. They touched her in a real, profound way, but she didn't know if she was strong enough to overcome the pain of her past. Her biggest fear had always been that she'd fall in love, but once a man saw the "real" her, he'd reject her like all the other guys she'd dated in the past.

"For the first time in my life, I know exactly what I want, and it's you…"

Sharleen read the expression on Emilio's face, saw the sincerity in his eyes, the truth, and caressed his cheek. She felt safe with him, cherished, and when they were apart he was all she should think of. His voice was soft, soothing, but Sharleen couldn't quiet her inner doubts. *Should I take another chance on love? Is Emilio worth it? Or am I just fooling myself?*

"I don't want you hooking up with other guys. I want us to be exclusive."

"What makes you think I'm dating other guys?" she asked, puzzled.

"Aren't you?"

"I don't have time to date. I'm too busy working."

His eyebrows merged, and he lowered his gaze in confusion. "And that's the truth?"

"Cross my heart and hope to die."

"I don't want to share you with anyone."

You won't have to. Besides, why would I want anyone else when I have you?

"Give me a chance to prove that I'm the right man for you." Emilio pointed a finger at his chest and flashed a boyish smile. "From now on just call me Mr. Right."

Her heart fluttered like a butterfly, and a smile overwhelmed her mouth. This time, Sharleen was the one who initiated the kiss. She closed her eyes and brushed her lips against his mouth. Lunch forgotten, she pleased him with her mouth, tongue and hands. She surprised herself by taking the reins, by being the aggressor, and when Emilio swept her up in his arms, Sharleen realized it was the only place in the world she wanted to be.

Chapter 11

"Thanks for coming with me to the hospital today," Jocelyn said, opening her handbag and rummaging around inside for her designer sunglasses. "I really appreciate it, and I know your visit meant a lot to my mom."

Sharleen smiled and joined her friend inside the elevator. "It was my pleasure. Your mom's a sweetheart, and I'm glad I could spend some time with her this afternoon."

As the elevator began its descent they chatted about their plans for the weekend.

"Do you want to go to the Atlanta job fair on Saturday?" Jocelyn asked.

Sharleen carefully considered her words. She wanted to tell Jocelyn about her plans with Emilio, but thought better of it. She couldn't risk one of her colleagues finding out about their secret trip to Miami and blabbing to Mrs. Fontaine. Her boss was busy promoting her new life-coaching book, *90 Days to a Better You*, which suited Sharleen fine. Image meant everything to Mrs. Fontaine, and she'd be furious if she discovered Sharleen had kissed Emilio.

You've done a lot more than just *kissing!* her conscience pointed out.

Her cheeks flushed with heat. For the past few weeks, she'd been hanging out with Emilio—playing tennis at his estate, watching movies in his home theater, sharing kisses under the stars—and every day their bond grew stronger. He'd welcomed her into his life, opened up to her, and she felt compelled to protect his privacy. Emilio was a quiet, sensitive man who enjoyed his solitude, and she didn't want to betray his trust by gossiping about their relationship to her friend.

"Sorry, Jocelyn, I can't. I'm busy this weekend."

"Do you work on Sunday, too?"

"Yes, I, um, have three consultations lined up and an afternoon session in Savannah."

"I am *so* jealous," she gushed, with a wistful look in her eyes. "I wish I had somewhere to go besides the hospital and the unemployment office."

"Keep your chin up. You'll find something soon. I know it."

"I sure hope so, because I'm tired of sitting at home waiting for the phone to ring."

The women exited the elevator and left the Atlanta Medical Center through the sliding glass doors. Hearing her iPhone chime, Sharleen pulled it out. The newest text message from Emilio made her heart soar.

I'm counting down the minutes until our flight to Miami. I'm going to wine you and dine you until you forget every other guy, and fall hopelessly in love with me...

Sharleen couldn't wipe the grin off her face, didn't even try. Emilio was a sweetheart, unlike anyone she'd ever met, and she adored everything about him—his boyish smile, his deep, throaty laugh, how his eyes twinkled at the corners when he was amused. He put her on a pedestal, treated her with kindness and respect and showered her with affection. *And he's an amazing kisser, too,* she thought, her mind overwhelmed with memories of their last date. *He makes me feel desirable, like the most beautiful woman in the world, and if I wasn't so self-conscious about my body, I'd want Emilio to be my—*

"I'm starving. Let's grab something to eat at that fast-food place across the street."

Making a mental note to return his text later, Sharleen put her cell phone away and turned to Jocelyn. "I don't want to eat fast food. Let's do dinner and a movie instead."

"I can't. I'm broke and unemployed, remember?"

"You haven't been job hunting long," she pointed out. "Give it more time."

"I've applied for dozens of positions, but no one's even called me for an interview." Sadness filled her eyes, and her bottom lip trembled. "I told my mom I'd help her out financially until she got back on her feet, and now that I'm unemployed, money's real tight."

"How much are your mom's medical bills?"

Jocelyn groaned. "Don't ask. I'm trying to stay positive, but every time I think about that notice of payment tacked to my fridge I feel nauseated."

Sharleen gave her a hug. It hurt to see her friend upset, so to cheer her up she said, "You're coming over tonight. We'll order pizza, make mocktails and watch movies."

"You're on, but no mocktails. The more tequila the better!"

After leaving the hospital, they stopped at the grocery store to stock up on food and drinks. They loaded the plastic bags into the car and set off for Inman Park. Driving across town, they sang along with the radio and reminisced about their early days at Pathways Center. It was hard for Sharleen to believe she'd known Jocelyn for five years, even harder for her to believe it had been almost a decade since her mom and dad died. *I wonder if my parents would have liked Emilio.*

Of course they would! her inner voice said. *What's not to like? He's considerate and thoughtful* and *he spoils you silly!* Jocelyn's cell phone rang, but she didn't answer it. "I have to change my number," she grumbled, hurling her iPhone into the bottom of her handbag. "Brad calls constantly, and it's driving me crazy. Why can't he leave me alone and go harass someone else?"

"Have you considered going to the authorities?"

"No, but I *have* considered hiring a hit man."

"Jocelyn, I'm serious—"

"So am I." Blinking back tears, she stared aimlessly out the windshield. "I still don't understand how this happened. I only had two glasses of wine the night we hooked up…"

Sharleen let Jocelyn vent, listened quietly as she recounted her story. Red flags went up, and a chilling thought entered her mind. "Did you leave your drink alone at any time? Was it ever out of your sight? Even for a second?"

"I don't remember. That night is such a blur."

"I think Brad spiked your drink. That's why you don't remember what happened—"

"No way. He's a chauvinistic pig, but he'd never do something *that* sneaky."

"Yes, he would," Sharleen insisted. "He took naked pictures of you and threatened to post them online. I wouldn't put anything past him. Guys like Brad are capable of anything."

"He didn't drug me, so drop it."

"Okay, okay, don't bite my head off. I won't mention it again."

Twenty minutes later, Sharleen parked in front of her brown two-story house. Inman Park was full of Victorian homes, trendy restaurants and boutiques, but what Sharleen loved most about the neighborhood were the people. Her neighbors smiled and waved as she got out of her car. Skateboarders zoomed down the street, and kids played hopscotch on the sidewalk. Laughter filled the air, and the smell of barbecue carried on the evening breeze.

Sharleen took the grocery bags out of the trunk, grabbed the letters in the mailbox and unlocked the front door. Sunshine streamed through the bay windows, filling the main floor with light. To create an inviting feel, she'd decorated with Persian area rugs, off-white furniture and brass lamps. Glass sculptures beautified end tables, and black-and-white photographs of her parents were prominently displayed in the foyer.

"Why don't you go in the living room and relax while I put away the groceries?"

"Sounds good to me." Jocelyn took a wine cooler out of the fridge and grabbed a pack of barbecue chips off the kitchen counter. "I'll order the pizza."

Working, attending aerobics classes and hanging out with Emilio left little time for housework, so while Jocelyn watched TV, Sharleen cleaned the kitchen and sorted through the mail. She was surprised to find a letter from Antwan's company, Elite Management. She ripped it open and read the handwritten note inside.

Keep up the good work, and there'll be more bonuses in your future.

Sharleen studied the check attached to the note, wondering if her eyes were deceiving her. Antwan had given her bonuses in the past, but he'd never sent her a check for ten thousand dollars. She grabbed her cell, dialed his number and when his answering machine came on left a message.

Her mind racing, she drummed her fingers on the counter. She had to return the check—it was the right thing to do, the only thing to do. Besides, she'd had nothing to do with Emilio's decision to come out of retirement, and she didn't want Antwan—or anyone else—to think she'd influenced him in any way. Emilio was his own man, his own boss, and if he ever found out about the bonus, he'd be upset.

Sharleen walked over to the garbage, but when her gaze fell across Jocelyn, she had second thoughts about destroying the check

An idea came to her. After grabbing a pen from her purse, she scrawled her signature on the back of the check and strode into the living room. "This is for you," she said excitedly, flopping down beside Jocelyn on the sofa. "Use it to pay your mom's medical bills."

"What's this?"

"A gift."

Reluctantly, Jocelyn took the check from her outstretched hand. "Ten thousand dollars?" Her hazel eyes grew wide. "I can't take your bonus. You earned it, not me."

"You need it more than I do."

She cocked her head to the right. "Did you win the lottery or something?"

"No, but I signed on to work with Rashad J, and the pay's incredible. We had our first session yesterday, and even though he's difficult, I'm up for the challenge."

Jocelyn squealed like a five-year-old girl at Disney World. "Rashad J! Wow, that's awesome. I love his new single, 'Heaven in Your Eyes.'"

Yeah, I like it, too. Every time I hear it on the radio, I think of Emilio.

"I'm so happy for you! Before you know it, you'll be *the* life coach to the stars, and celebrities will be beating down your door for a private session."

"I don't want to be famous. I just want to help my clients discover their life's purpose," Sharleen said, speaking from the heart.

"I don't know when I'll be able to pay you back. It could be months from now."

"Jocelyn, it's a gift. No strings attached."

Her lips moved soundlessly, and unshed tears filled her eyes. "I can't believe this. Yesterday, I didn't know how I was going to pay my mom's medical bills, and now I have enough money to pay off the balance."

"You've been an amazing friend and colleague, and this is my way of saying thank you."

"I love you, girl. You're the best."

The doorbell rang, and Jocelyn jumped to her feet.

"I'll pay for the pizza," she said, with a cheeky grin. "It's the *least* I can do!"

Sharleen picked up the remote control and flipped channels. On the sports channel she saw a commercial for the World Series Racing All-Star Race, and she leaned forward in her seat. Her eyes were glued to the picture on the screen of Emilio. His five o'clock shadow and brooding gaze gave him a mysterious air, and he looked drop-dead sexy in his red-and-white fitted coveralls. He'd been training with his team for weeks, and Sharleen was surprised by the changes in his personality. He smiled more, laughed more and constantly cracked jokes about his grumpy pit-crew boss.

"Girl, get in here quick!"

Startled by the urgency in Jocelyn's tone, Sharleen raced into the foyer. The first thing she noticed was all the shopping bags on the floor; the second was the wide-eyed expression on her friend's face. "What's going on?" Sharleen asked, dumbfounded.

"A delivery guy just brought all this inside and sped off in his truck. I tried to get his name, but he was gone in the blink of an eye."

"Where did all these bags come from?"

Jocelyn pointed at the shiny purple logo on the top of the garment bags. "Fashion Starr, of course! And it looks like someone bought you their entire summer collection!"

Sharleen crouched and peeked inside the shopping bags. Jocelyn was right; there were thousands of dollars' worth of designer clothes, shoes and accessories.

The high-end boutique catered to socialites with money to burn—and tiny waistlines—so she was shocked to discover all of the outfits were in her size.

With Jocelyn's help, she carried the bags into her bedroom and dumped them on the bed.

"I feel like I've died and gone to retail heaven!" Jocelyn joked, carefully admiring each article of clothing. She picked up a striped, one-shoulder bathing suit and whistled. "Wow, this is *some* suit. You're going to be the sexiest woman at the beach this summer…"

Her thoughts returned to the conversation she'd had with Emilio, weeks earlier, about their trip to Miami, and Sharleen knew, without a doubt, that Emilio was behind the gift.

He'd gone to Fashion Starr, selected the clothes and arranged to have them delivered to her house.

Her gaze strayed to the clock on her nightstand. She wanted to call Emilio to thank him for the presents, but since she didn't want Jocelyn to hear their conversation, she decided to phone him later, after she dropped her friend at home.

"I knew Antwan had a crush on you, but I didn't realize he liked you *this* much."

"Antwan didn't buy the clothes. Emilio Morretti did."

"The Italian race-car driver you're coaching?"

Sharleen nodded, hid the smile threatening to explode onto her lips. "The one and only."

"Holy Hannah!"

Jocelyn leaped to her feet, gripped Sharleen's shoulders and shook her like a rag doll. "Why didn't you tell me you were dating a living legend? How long has this been going on? Is Emilio a good kisser? Do you think he could be the one?"

Yes, and the more time we spend together the more I love him.

"Start talking," Jocelyn ordered. "I want to hear everything."

"Emilio's not my boyfriend—"

"Your eyes light up when you say his name."

"I'm thrilled about the progress he's made the past couple months, that's all," she said, avoiding her friend's gaze. "Our first few sessions were rough, but now he's opening up more, attending group therapy sessions and even reading self-help books."

"You've got the hots for him. It's written all over your face."

"I want to help Emilio overcome the pain of his past and give him the necessary tools to move forward in life. Sleeping with him is the furthest thing from my mind."

Liar! her inner voice yelled. *It's the* only *thing on your mind, and you know it!*

"Does he know that you're—"

"No, and I'm not going to tell him." Sharleen struggled with her words, but after a few moments of quiet deliberation, she spoke from the heart. "I'm scared if I tell Emilio the truth, he'll run for the hills, and I don't want to lose him. He's an amazing guy, and I love spending time with him."

"Well, the feeling is definitely mutual," Jocelyn said, gesturing to the shopping bags covering the queen-size bed. "Look at all this stuff. Emilio's trying to impress you, and for good reason. You're a terrific girl, and I knew it was just a matter of time before a rich, handsome guy swept you off your pretty little feet."

Was Jocelyn right? Was it possible Emilio had fallen for her, too?

"I'm happy for you, but be careful. I don't want you to get—"

"I know, I know, you don't have to say it." She rolled her eyes to the ceiling. "Emilio's out of my league, and he'll only end up hurting me in the end."

"That's not what I was going to say. If Mrs. Fontaine finds out you're dating a client, she'll fire you, so be careful who you confide in about Emilio."

The doorbell rang, and Jocelyn whooped for joy.

"Finally! I thought the pizza would never get here," she said, laughing. "I'll be right back."

Sharleen watched Jocelyn leave, then swiped her cell phone off the dresser and went into the bathroom. She locked the door and dialed Emilio's number. He answered on the first ring, and the moment she heard his voice the smile in her heart spread to her lips. *His accent is the sexiest thing I've ever heard, and every time he says my name I melt.*

"I was just thinking of you," he said smoothly. "Do you like your new Miami wardrobe?"

"Yes, of course, thank you, but I wish you hadn't gone to the trouble."

"It was no trouble at all. You're important to me, and I wanted you to feel special."

"Well, you certainly succeeded in doing that. I feel like Julia Roberts in *Pretty Woman*."

"Great. Mission accomplished!"

They laughed together.

"I miss you," he said, his voice a sensuous whisper. "Come over tonight."

"I can't. I have company."

"I told you I don't want to share you with other guys."

"Emilio, relax. I'm hanging out with Jocelyn, not Leonardo DiCaprio!"

He laughed, scolded her for being a smart-ass and vowed to get even. "I'm excited about our trip to Miami, and I hope you are, too…"

I am, but I'm nervous about our sleeping arrangements.

"Are you all packed and ready to go?" he asked.

"I'll finish packing tomorrow after work."

"I thought you were taking the day off?"

"I can't. Channel 6 News is doing a feature story on Mrs. Fontaine, and she wants staff on hand for pictures and interviews."

"I'm picking you up at six. Don't forget. And pack everything I bought you."

"Okay, pops, I will," she drawled, unable to resist poking fun at him.

"I *love it* when you call me Big Poppa!"

Sharleen cracked up, laughed so hard tears spilled down her cheeks.

When they ended the phone call, she joined Jocelyn in the kitchen, but thoughts of Emilio remained. From the very beginning she'd known there was something special about him. It was the way he spoke to her, his chivalrous, old-fashioned ways and his gentle nature. He never raised his voice, never lost his cool and treated everyone—from his butler to his gardener—with respect. And as Sharleen sat at the kitchen table, sipping her cocktail, she wondered if she'd be able to resist him in Miami.

Chapter 12

Sharleen rose from her desk, spent a few minutes stretching her tired, aching muscles and strode out of her office. Since arriving at Pathways that morning, she'd been working nonstop, and this was her only chance to take a break before her three o'clock session. Most of her colleagues had left for the day, and the few who remained were in the reception area chatting about their plans for the Memorial Day weekend. The center was infused with sunlight, the air smelled of freshly brewed coffee and the framed quotes hanging on the walls invigorated her.

Sharleen caught sight of the clock hanging above the fish tank, and her thoughts turned to Emilio. They were leaving for Miami that evening, and after a long, stressful week, she was looking forward to having some fun in the sun. She'd packed yesterday, but still had misgivings about wearing the outfits Emilio had bought her. *What if people stare? What if they point at me? And most importantly, what will Emilio think when he sees my—*

"I can't do this anymore. It's too stressful," said a female voice from inside the staff room.

Frowning, she stopped abruptly in the hallway. She wondered if one of her colleagues was having an emotional breakdown. It happened more often than her boss cared to admit, and these days nothing that happened at Pathways Center surprised her.

Sharleen knew it was wrong to eavesdrop, but she leaned against the staff-room door and listened for several minutes.

"It's not over until *I* say it's over, and if you tell Mrs. Fontaine about us, I'll post naked pictures of you online. Don't tempt me. I'll do it."

"You can't," a high-pitched voice wailed. "My parents are ministers pastoring in Augusta. They'd be mortified."

"Then do what I say, or else."

Enraged, Sharleen threw open the door and stalked inside. Brad was in the kitchen with his back to her, and a buxom intern with curly brown hair was cornered against the microwave stand.

Her eyes narrowed, zeroed in on him with acute precision. He had one hand inside the intern's blouse, the other underneath her skirt and his mouth against her neck. "Let her go."

The intern gasped and jumped in the air. Wiping her tearstained cheeks, she straightened her clothes and fled the room as if her life was in grave danger.

"What's up?" Brad wore an arch grin. "I didn't see you there."

"I'm going to report you to the human-resources department for—"

"There's nothing to tell. I came in here to grab a drink." He gestured to the coffee mug on the table. Beside it was an iPhone, a stack of envelopes and a BLT sandwich. "Focus on doing your job, not stirring up malicious gossip."

"When Mrs. Fontaine finds out you're harassing female staff, she'll fire you."

"No, she won't. I have more celebrity clients than anyone else, and thanks to me, the center has grown in leaps and bounds the past nine years. And," he said, his tone dripping with pride, "I'm a shoo-in for the vice-president position."

Sharleen rolled her eyes. She couldn't believe his nerve, his complete and utter disregard for everyone.

"I have things to do and people to see," he boasted. "See you around, toots."

"Off to terrorize another intern?" she said, too angry to bite her tongue.

"If you must know, I'm off to meet Zoe Archer-Ross at her Brookhaven mansion." He adjusted his marine-blue tie and buttoned his suit jacket. "Since your friend was dumb enough to get fired, I took on all of her old clients. It sucks to be Jocelyn, but it's great to be me!"

As she stood there, listening to Brad bad-mouth her best friend, she had to resist punching him in the face. He deserved no less for what he'd done to Jocelyn. She'd have the last laugh, though. No doubt about it. Once she landed the VP position, she was getting rid of him once and for all, and no one was going to stop her.

"How's Jocelyn doing?" He cocked an eyebrow and licked his lips suggestively. "I should swing by her place later. I bet she'd like that."

"You're delusional. You're the last person she wants to see."

"And you're jealous. I have girlfriends in every county, and you have no one."

You're wrong. I have Emilio, and he's all the man I need.

"You wish you had a man like me," he bragged. "I'm the kind of lover women dream about. Ask Jocelyn."

"That's not what I heard." Sharleen struggled to keep a straight face. "Erectile dysfunction is nothing to be ashamed of, Brad. There's help available. My aunt Phyllis is a urologist with decades of experience helping impotent men like you. Do you want her business card?"

His face fell, and the grin slid off his mouth.

"Stop harassing Jocelyn, or we'll go to the police and file a complaint."

"What for?"

"You drugged her and lured her into bed."

"That's a lie," he argued, his voice a nervous squeak. "We had consensual sex."

Curling her hands into fists, she stared him down. "I don't think the new *female* district attorney will see it that way. She's tough on crime, and after she hears Jocelyn's heartbreaking story, you'll be booked so fast it'll make your head spin."

"It's her word against mine, and I have friends in high places."

"A hair-follicle test will prove she's telling the truth."

Brad tugged at the collar of his dress shirt.

"You're looking at serious charges and years be-hind bars." Sharleen saw the color drain from his face, the flicker of fear that flashed in his eyes. She knew, without a doubt, that her suspicions were true. "Leave Jocelyn alone, or she'll go to the cops."

Her legs felt like rubber, but she marched toward the door. Without warning, Brad grabbed her arm and slid in front of her. He looked out of it, like a crazed man with nothing to lose. His nostrils were flaring, his face was quivering with rage and he was shouting his words. "Who the hell do you think you are? You think you're better than me, but you're not..."

Panic welled up inside her, made it impossible to breathe, to think. Self-preservation kicked in, and she wrestled her arm away. Sharleen stepped on Brad's foot and broke free of his fierce grip. He staggered back into the table like a drunk and knocked over his mug. Coffee drenched everything on the table and dripped onto the floor.

Brad yelped, as if he'd been bitten by a dog. "You stupid bitch!" he shouted, scooping up his dripping cell phone. He ran into the kitchen, wiped it with a dish towel and tapped the screen. "It won't work! You destroyed it!"

The door flew open, and Mrs. Fontaine stalked inside. "Brad, what's going on?" she asked. "I can hear you shouting from the other side of the building, and so can the crew from Channel 6 News. Are you trying to embarrass me?"

"It's not my fault." Brad raised his iPhone. "That stupid bitch destroyed my cell phone!"

Mrs. Fontaine narrowed her eyes and propped her

hands on her hips. "I won't tolerate this kind of behavior at my clinic."

"You don't understand," he argued.

"You owe Ms. Nichols an apology."

Brad scoffed. "Like hell I do."

Tension filled the room, and a long, awkward silence followed. No one spoke, and as the seconds ticked by, Sharleen wondered if Brad's outburst was going to cost him his job. *I sure hope so!* she thought, glancing from her enemy to her boss. *Brad's an embarrassment to this company, and he doesn't deserve to be a life coach.*

"Pathways Center is a safe, peaceful environment, and I won't allow you to abuse my staff and clients." Mrs. Fontaine spoke calmly, as if she were in complete control, but her face was covered in anger. "I'd like to have a word with you in my office to discuss this matter further."

Brad stalked out of the room, mumbling to himself, and Sharleen released the breath she'd been holding. Before she could even think of what to say to smooth things over with her boss, Mrs. Fontaine rested an arm on her shoulder and said, "I'm sorry about that. Brad's behavior was completely uncalled for, and I want you to know I am taking this matter very seriously."

"Thank you, Mrs. Fontaine."

"Will you be around this evening? I'd like to hear your side of the story."

"No, I, um, have an eight o'clock session with Emilio Morretti," she said, the white lie rolling smoothly off her tongue. Her contract had ended with him yesterday, so technically she wasn't his life coach anymore, but the less her boss knew about their relationship the better. "He wants to discuss renewing our contract. Do you want me to cancel?"

"No, of course not. Mr. Morretti is an important client, and I don't want to disappoint him. We'll talk one day next week."

Sharleen felt her cell phone vibrate inside her blazer, but she didn't answer until Mrs. Fontaine turned and left the staff room. It was Emilio, and hearing his voice instantly calmed her nerves. He sounded relaxed, as if he were stretched out by his pool sipping a glass of merlot. The image of him in swim trunks made her mouth dry. "Hi, Emilio," she said, suddenly feeling upbeat. "How are you?"

"Terrible. I miss you."

"I saw you on Tuesday, remember? We had dinner at Restaurant Eugene."

"I know, but it feels like I haven't seen you in weeks."

"You're so dramatic," she teased, with a laugh. "You should consider a career in movies, Mr. Morretti. You're *quite* the actor."

"And you're *quite* the beauty."

"Flattery will get you everywhere," Sharleen said, in a singsong voice.

"Will it help me win your heart?"

Goose bumps tickled her skin, and her pulse roared in her ears. Sharleen wished she could stay on the phone with Emilio, but she had to warn Jocelyn about Brad. There was a good chance he'd show up at her house unannounced, and she wanted to give her friend a heads-up. "I have to go," she said, apologetically. "I have an important call to make."

"I'll be at your place by six. Don't forget to pack your bathing suit."

"How can I forget when you keep reminding me?"

Emilio chuckled. "'Bye, gorgeous. See you in a few."

Emilio hung up and put his cell phone into his shirt pocket. His smile couldn't be any bigger, any brighter. Having Sharleen in his life made him feel invigorated, as if he could do anything. Emilio was anxious to see her, ready to finally kick off their romantic weekend, but he had an important stop to make before he picked her up. *I hope Sharleen loves flowers, because I'm going to have dozens of roses delivered to our cottage at the Fisher Island Club.*

Standing, he swiped his car keys off the dresser and jogged downstairs to the main floor. As he reached the foyer, he saw his sister enter the house through the front door using her key. All dolled up like a pop princess, her glittery eye makeup, pink jumpsuit and sky-high heels screamed for attention. "I got here just in the nick of time," Francesca said, whipping off her Prada sunglasses. "We can talk during the drive to the track."

Emilio gave his sister a hug and a kiss on each cheek. "I don't have practice today. I'm flying to Miami tonight for the Exotic Car Show."

"I *love* South Beach. Do you want some company?"

Yes, that's why I invited Sharleen to join me. This is my chance to prove myself to her, to show her how much she means to me, and I'm going to pull out all the stops to make her mine.

"No, not this time." Emilio picked up his suitcase, activated the alarm and led his sister outside. The sky was overcast, threatening rain, but it didn't dampen his good mood "I have to go, but I'll call you when I get back to town. We can have dinner."

"Are you staying at Nicco's estate?"

"He offered, but I turned him down. He's a newly-wed, and I don't want to intrude."

"Are you traveling alone?"

Pretending he didn't hear the question, Emilio stalked into his ten-car garage and flipped the lights on. He unlocked the doors of his Escalade and tossed his suitcase into the trunk. His SUV was gleaming, buffed to a shine, and remembering the last time he'd had Sharleen in his car made a devilish grin fill his lips.

Images of Tuesday night teased his mind. Stealing kisses during dinner, walking hand in hand through Centennial Olympic Park, making out like teenagers in the backseat of his SUV. They'd spent hours talking about their trip to Miami, their hopes and dreams for the future, and when they kissed good-night, he'd felt closer to her than ever before.

"Ginger said she spotted you and that life-coach girl downtown a couple days ago," Francesca said coolly, her tone filled with accusation. "She said you guys looked like a couple."

That's because we are. And Sharleen's not a girl; she's a vibrant, passionate woman who means the world to me.

"I have a flight to catch. We'll talk when I get back."

"Can I get a small loan?" Francesca touched his arm and gazed up at him adoringly, as if her heart was bursting with love. "I promise to pay you back as soon as I get my first paycheck."

He raised an eyebrow. "You got a job? Where?"

"At Elite Management. Antwan's assistant quit last

week, so he asked me to fill in for the rest of the month. Answering phones and fetching coffee isn't really my thing, but I *love* meeting his celebrity clients, especially the sexy athletes worth millions!"

Emilio chuckled and shook his head at his sister.

"All I need is five thousand dollars. I'm throwing a birthday party for Ginger, and I need to give the caterer the deposit in the morning."

"Francesca, we discussed this."

"We did?" she asked. "I don't remember."

"If you decide to go to college, or enroll in beauty school, I'll pay your tuition, but I won't fund your extravagant lifestyle anymore." Emilio paused and took a moment to regroup so he didn't lose his temper. Over the years, he'd spoken to his sister several times about her outrageous spending, but it wasn't until a recent coaching session with Sharleen that he'd had a light-bulb moment. If he didn't stop indulging Francesca, she'd never grow up. He felt responsible for Lucca's death, and buying her expensive gifts used to make him feel better, but not anymore. Those days were behind him. He was sick of being a human ATM machine and had to put his foot down.

"Francesca, enough is enough. You can't keep living like this. You'll be twenty-six in a few months, but you're still acting like a teenager."

"All I've ever wanted was to be a mom, but now that Lucca's gone…" Her voice broke, cracked with emotion. "He was my world, and life seems meaningless without him."

I used to feel that way, too, but then I met Sharleen, and my life changed for the better.

At the thought of her, he felt a sudden rush of adrenaline. Introducing her to his pit crew last Friday had been a huge step for him, but she'd easily won them over with her easygoing nature and infectious laugh. Until meeting her, he'd never considered getting married or having children, but these days it was all he could think about. But before he could pop the question, and move Sharleen into his estate, he had to win her heart.

"Sometimes I think about moving back to Italy," Francesca continued, "but I think I'd miss living in the States too much. I honestly don't know what I want. I'm so confused…"

Emilio kissed her on the forehead and rubbed her shoulders. "I'm going to arrange for you to have a private coaching session with Sharleen here at the house. She's the best in the business, and I'm confident she can help you discover your purpose in life."

"And *I* think she's after your money."

Oh, brother, not this *again.*

"That life-coach girl told you to cut me off financially, didn't she?"

"Sharleen had nothing to do with my decision. I love you, and I'm here to support you—"

"You have a funny way of showing it." Francesca poked out her bottom lip. "Why are you being unreasonable? It's just five thousand dollars. That's chump change to you."

"That's not the point."

"Whatever. Forget I asked."

Emilio felt his heart soften and his resolve crumble. He put his hand in his back pocket to retrieve his wallet. He'd give Francesca the money, but insist she pay him back.

Yeah, right! You have a better chance of meeting the president!

"You used to have my back, and now I don't know who you are anymore," Francesca said.

Nose in the air, she stepped past him and stomped off. He watched with a heavy heart as she stormed down the cobblestone walkway. He called out to her, told her to come back, but she ignored him. Francesca jumped into her Mercedes-Benz convertible—the one he'd bought her for Christmas—and tore through the gates of his estate like a bat out of hell.

Chapter 13

South Beach, the infamous Miami district Sharleen had seen on TV and read about in magazines, lived up to its hype. Latin music blared from bars, and the air smelled of tantalizing aromas. Street performers entertained tourists, and fabulously gorgeous people cruised down the block in luxury vehicles with personalized license plates. Excited to be in such a vibrant city, she shielded her eyes from the hot, blistering sun and soaked in the world around her.

"Are you having a good time?" Emilio asked, resting a hand on her back.

"I shouldn't have let you talk me into going in-line skating." Sharleen lowered her shoulders and swung her arms to increase her speed. "I haven't done this in years."

"Don't sweat it. You're doing great."

Yeah, until I trip and fall flat on my face!

They'd arrived at the Fisher Island Club last night, and after checking out their cozy, two-bedroom cottage, they'd set out on foot to explore the secluded island getaway. Unbeknownst to her, Emilio had arranged for them to have a private cooking lesson with reality star chef Chaz Romero and a candlelit dinner on the beach. His thoughtfulness made her desire him even more, and they'd laughed the night away over filet mignon and Italian wine. They'd laughed and kissed and danced in the moonlight to the distant sound of Latin music. Emilio made her feel cherished and adored, as if she mattered to him more than anything. It was a heady feeling, one she'd never experienced before.

"I'm not used to skating ten miles in ninety-degree temperatures."

He raised an eyebrow. "You could have fooled me. You're a natural."

Sharleen skated over to one of the picnic tables at South Pointe Park, sat down and fanned a hand to her face. "I need a break and a cold drink."

"Coming right up," he said, kissing her on the forehead. "Wait here. I'll be back in a few."

Her eyes followed him, moved over his chiseled physique with deliberate slowness. Emilio skated over to the food truck parked on the sidewalk and joined the slow-moving line. Like vultures, a group of bikini-clad women crowded around him, batting their eyelashes.

Sharleen shot evil daggers at the young, perky quartet. Emilio couldn't go anywhere in Miami without females asking him for his autograph or slipping him a phone number when they *thought* Sharleen wasn't looking. They'd spent the morning exploring art galleries and museums, and everywhere she turned women were undressing him with their eyes. It was annoying, and although he never gave her reason to feel insecure, she was. His admirers had perfect skin and great bodies, and Sharleen couldn't help envying their gorgeous looks.

"You look handsome on TV, but you're even sexier in person," she overheard the redhead say. "I've seen all of your races, and I've always dreamed of meeting you…"

Sharleen scoffed, rolled her eyes. She wanted to take off her skates and fling them at the redhead, but she didn't want to get arrested for assault with a deadly weapon.

"Since we're in South Beach, I figured we could try some of the local cuisine…"

Sharleen blinked and stared up at Emilio. He looked smokin' hot in his aviator sunglasses, navy polo shirt and cargo shorts, but it was his strong, masculine cologne that aroused her. It overpowered her senses, made her thoughts take an erotic detour. X-rated images consumed her mind, but she kept her hands in her lap and off of his chest. "Something smells delicious," she said. "What did you buy?"

"The works. Ceviche, Cuban sandwiches, fruit salad and sangria iced tea."

"I said I wanted a cold drink, not a buffet lunch!"

"Eat up. You'll need your strength for what I have planned for you later."

She hid her nervous excitement and sipped her sangria. As they ate lunch, they discussed how to spend the rest of the afternoon, the Exotic Car Show and their evening dinner plans.

"I'm a bit nervous about meeting your cousin and his wife," Sharleen confessed.

"Don't be. Nicco's a great guy." Emilio finished his sandwich and then cleaned his mouth with a napkin. "I haven't met Jariah yet, or her six-year-old daughter, but I've heard nothing but good things. Nicco adores Ava and treats her like his own flesh and blood."

"Where do they live?"

"In Coral Gables, but they'll meet us at the Exotic Car Show and we'll drive to their estate together..." His gaze left her face, and he broke off speaking.

Sharleen glanced over her shoulder, expecting to see a pretty blonde behind her, but she was surprised to see dozens of elementary schoolchildren playing soccer. They ran down the field, shrieking and laughing, and their high-pitched voices filled the air.

"Lucca would have turned seven on August first."

Sharleen stood, came around the picnic table and sat down beside him. She clasped his hand and stroked his forearms. "Are you still having nightmares about the accident?"

"Not every night." Emilio wore a sad smile. "You were right. Meditation *does* work."

They sat in silence, sipping their drinks and watching the kids play soccer.

"I replay the accident in my mind every day, but I still don't understand why Lucca died. He was only five years old. He had his entire life ahead of him."

His eyes were downcast, his shoulders bent, and when he spoke, his voice was filled with sorrow. "I want to tell you what happened. Maybe it will help me heal and bring us even closer together."

Sharleen nodded to encourage him.

"I was in my office, reviewing film tapes with my crew, when Lucca burst in and jumped into my arms. He was running around, getting into everything, so I sent him to his room so he wouldn't disturb us. But instead of going upstairs, he went outside."

Dread flooded her body, and her throat closed up.

"We found him an hour later, facedown in the pool. He wasn't breathing, so I did CPR until the paramedics arrived… I prayed that he'd pull through, but he didn't."

Words didn't come. Her thoughts were clouded with sadness, and it took everything in her not to break down. Her heart broke for Emilio, and finally after weeks of intense coaching sessions, she understood why he blamed himself for his nephew's death.

"I should have been watching *him* instead of film tape, but I was so stressed-out about my upcoming race in Barcelona that I wasn't thinking straight." He turned his head away and wiped at his eyes with the back of his hand. "I was so obsessed with fame and fortune and my stupid legacy that I let it consume me, and it cost me Lucca."

Emilio stared out onto the field, as if he were lost in another world. Minutes passed, and the longer the silence dragged on, the more helpless Sharleen felt.

"I am so sorry for your loss." Sharleen paused to gather her thoughts. She racked her mind for something insightful to say, for the perfect quote to comfort him, but came up empty. "I wish there was something I could say to make you feel better."

"You already have." He faced her and stared deep in her eyes.

"I didn't think I deserved to be happy, but then I met you and I realized I'd been given a second chance. And this time around I'm going to help others, not obsess over money and fame."

Entranced by the sound of his voice, she moved closer to him, eager to hear more. In her peripheral vision, she saw something orange flapping in the sky and glanced at it. An airplane, towing a wide banner, flew overhead, drawing everyone's attention. Sharleen Nichols Is the Most Beautiful Woman in South Beach.

Sharleen gasped and cupped a hand over her mouth. Her heartbeat roared in her ears, pounded so fast she couldn't catch her breath. Emilio had surprised her again, when she least expected it. She was blown away by the romantic, unexpected gesture. Yesterday, he'd filled her room at the Fisher Island Club with dozens of roses and treated her to a dream date on the beach. He was a modern-day Prince Charming, and there was never a dull moment when he was around.

"Oh, my gosh, this is insane!" she said, her eyes glued to the banner. "I can't believe you did this!"

"I've fallen hard for you, Sharleen, and I want the world to know."

His caress along the small of her back flooded her body with heat. Leaning forward until their heads were touching, he stroked her cheeks with his fingertips. The baby-fine hairs on her neck shot up, and a delicious tingle zipped down her spine.

"How do you feel about moving our coaching sessions from the office to the bedroom?" he asked, his voice a husky whisper. "I know what I want, and it's you."

Sharleen didn't trust herself to speak. There was so much she wanted to say, but she didn't know where to begin. Her tongue felt numb, but she forced the truth out of her mouth. "Emilio, there are things about me you don't know."

"You're not an ax murderer, are you?"

Despite herself, she laughed at his joke.

"There is nothing you could say that will change the way I feel about you."

That's what they all say until they find out the truth.

"And no one has to know that we're dating. It'll be our little secret."

"Then I can't renew your contract. It would be wrong and unethical, and it could cost me my job." An idea sparked in her mind, one Sharleen wished she'd thought of sooner.

"My former colleague, Jocelyn Calhoun, taught me everything I know about life coaching, and she's one of the smartest, most insightful people I know. Would you be willing to meet her?"

"Sure, why not? She sounds like good people."

"No funny business, Emilio."

He wore an innocent face and held up his palms as if he were surrendering to the cops. "What are you talking about? I'm as good as they come."

"No flirting, no long lunches at Dolce Vita, and I don't care how hot it is outside—keep your shirt on at all times. Got it?"

"You have nothing to worry about. I don't want anyone but you." He cupped her chin in his hands and lowered his mouth to hers. "Now shut up and kiss me."

Chapter 14

The Fisher Island Club, a world-class resort accessible only by ferry, was *the* hotel to the stars and the most breathtaking place Sharleen had ever seen. Exiting the luxury yacht, hand in hand with Emilio, she marveled at the beauty of her surroundings. She took in the lush grounds, the exotic birds perched high in the coconut palms and the stunning view of the Atlantic Ocean. Celebrities were everywhere—tanning on the beach, sipping cocktails at the bar, snapping selfies in the turquoise blue water, but Sharleen only had eyes for Emilio. He'd been doting on her ever since they'd arrived in Miami, and every time he called her his Island Beauty she wanted to do cartwheels up and down the beach.

Emilio hugged her close to his side, and joy swelled inside her chest. They'd had the perfect day, one she'd never forget. They'd had a buffet-style breakfast in their private courtyard, played three rounds of golf with the newest Hollywood "It" couple and toured the island aboard an eighty-foot yacht. It amazed Sharleen how much they had in common, how much they'd laughed and how he'd opened up to her about his family. No topic was off-limits, no question too personal, and hearing about how his relatives had cashed in on his grief after his nephew's death made Sharleen want to strangle his estranged relatives.

"Did you have fun? I know the tour guide was a bit eccentric, but I learned a lot from him."

"I did, too, and now I understand why locals call Fisher Island the playground of the rich and famous." Sharleen snapped pictures of the tropical garden with her camera phone and uploaded the images to her Instagram page. "The resort has everything a girl could want. Watch out, Emilio—I may *never* leave!"

"That's fine with me. As long as I have you by my side, I'll be happy."

Touched by his words, Sharleen smiled and snuggled against his shoulder. She wanted to jump into his arms and shower his face with kisses, but she exercised self-control and squeezed his hand instead.

Emilio led Sharleen inside the sunlit atrium and signed an autograph for the manager's teenage son at the front desk. "I didn't realize it was four thirty," he said. "We better head back to the cottage and get ready."

"For what? I thought we were staying in tonight." Sharleen gave him a puzzled look, but deep down she was thrilled that he'd planned something special for her and was curious to know exactly what it was. "Where are we going?"

He kissed her on the cheek. "Be patient. You'll find out soon enough."

An hour later, Sharleen was showered and dressed. They were sharing the cottage, but they had separate rooms. Wanting to look great for Emilio, she'd taken extra care doing her hair and makeup, but despite her efforts, she still felt frumpy and unattractive. She stared at the walk-in closet, wishing she could wear one of the outfits he'd bought her instead of her boring gray cardigan and floral-print dress. But she feared he'd take one look at her in the white backless dress and bolt from their suite.

Hearing a knock on the door, she grabbed her purse off the bed and hustled across the room. The cottage had all the comforts of home and reminded Sharleen of a property she'd once seen on an episode of *Lifestyles of the Rich and Famous.*

"Sharleen, are you ready? The limo just pulled up."

Her palms were slick with sweat, but she opened the door and strode into the living room. Emilio switched off the TV and turned to face her. Disappointment flickered in his eyes, and his smile looked forced, as if it required every ounce of his strength. Hurt by his reaction, her shoulders sagged, and her spirits fell.

"You don't like my outfit," she said quietly, fighting back tears. Crying was completely out of character, but his rejection stung. Emilio was important to her, and she always wanted to look her best for him. "I'll go change."

His face softened. "Don't be silly. You look great. You always do."

"I'm a big girl. I can handle it, so just spit it out. What's wrong with my outfit?"

"Nothing, if you're going to Bible study."

She didn't join in his laughter.

"Don't you like the outfits I bought for you?" he asked.

"Yes, of course, but they're too revealing for me. I prefer more conservative looks."

"You have a great figure. You should show it off sometimes." He winked, and a grin dimpled his cheek. "Especially when you're in Miami with me."

"Emilio, I'm not one of your model ex-girlfriends. You can't expect me to—"

"Thank God for that," he drawled, with a sigh of relief. "I've dated a lot of famous women, but none of them can hold a candle to you. You're in a league of your own."

I am? Sharleen found herself lost in the allure of his voice and his piercing gaze. It took all of her effort not to jump into his arms and kiss him all over. The more he spoke, complimenting and praising her, the more she desired him.

"You're genuine and considerate, and you don't give a damn about my celebrity status. That's just one of the many things I love about you. You always have my best interest at heart, and I trust you wholeheartedly."

Love? The word reverberated in her mind, made her dizzy and weak in the knees. Afraid her legs were going to buckle, she leaned against the mahogany desk for support. Was it true? Did Emilio love her? Or was this just a ploy to get her into bed?

"I want to show you off tonight." His voice was a low, sensuous whisper, and lust shone in his eyes.

"You're gorgeous, and I want the whole world to know that you're my girl."

"Stop saying that. It isn't true… I'm not like other girls… I'm different."

Emilio stared at her as if she were speaking a foreign language. "What are you talking about? You're beautiful inside and out."

She couldn't look at him, didn't dare meet his gaze for fear of bursting into tears.

He clasped her hand, led her over to the leather reading chair in front of the window and pulled her down onto his lap. They sat in silence for several minutes, listening to birds squawk, the soothing sounds of the ocean and the raucous volleyball game happening on the beach.

"You're shaking." Emilio wrapped his arms around her and whispered in her ear, "Tell me what's bothering you. I want to help."

I can't. You won't understand. No one ever *does!*

"Who convinced you that you're unworthy of love? Was it an abusive ex-boyfriend?"

Sharleen dropped her gaze to her lap and tugged at the sleeve of her cardigan.

"I'm not letting you go until we talk, so if you want to have dinner at the best Cajun restaurant in Miami, you better start talking."

His joke, and the sympathetic expression on his face, eased the tension, lightened the mood. Still, she didn't speak. Her head hurt, and her stomach was curled into knots. Reluctantly, her heart pounding with fear, she took off her sweater. To her relief, Emilio didn't gasp or recoil in disgust at the sight of her scars.

"The doctors at Grady Memorial Hospital said it

was a miracle I survived the fire, but when I saw the burns on my body, I wanted to die. I felt ugly, and I couldn't look in the mirror for weeks."

Anguish filled his eyes. "You were in the house fire that killed your parents?"

"I feel asleep on the couch watching a movie and when I woke up the house was filled with smoke." Bitter memories crowded her mind, overwhelming her with sadness. A chill whipped through the room, and she hugged her arms to her chest to ward off the cold. "I tried to crawl to the door, but it was hard to breathe, and I couldn't find my way out. A firefighter found me unconscious in the hallway and carried me outside to the ambulance."

"You're the most courageous woman I know, and hearing your story makes me respect and admire you even more."

Tears pricked her eyes, but she conquered her emotions and spoke openly, without fear or restraint. She told Emilio about the weeks she'd spent in the hospital, her bouts with depression during her recovery and her disastrous dating history. "Men want perfection, and I'm not it," she said sadly. "I got tired of being disappointed by the opposite sex, so I decided to focus on my career instead of my love life."

"It sounds like you've given up on ever finding Mr. Right. Does that mean I don't stand a chance?"

This time Sharleen laughed, and it felt good. A weight had been lifted from her shoulders, and now that Emilio knew the truth about her past she didn't have to hide anymore. Knowing that he cared about her, in spite of her physical imperfections, meant everything to her.

"Have you ever been in love?" he asked.

The question caught her off guard, and several seconds passed before she regained her voice. "Yes, once, a long time ago, but I was young and foolish. It didn't mean anything."

"I'd like to hear about it." His smile was full of sympathy and understanding. "What happened?"

Her heart ached when she remembered her sophomore year at Duke University. She wanted to change the subject, but knew there was no point trying to pull a fast one on Emilio. In the end, he'd persuade her to open up to him, so why bother? He radiated warmth and compassion, and Sharleen felt so at ease with him, so comfortable in his arms.

"I met Jarvis at the campus library, and we immediately hit it off. He was outgoing, from a great family and an old soul like me."

Emilio leaned into her, tightened his hold around her waist.

"Five months later, we were talking about moving in together and eloping after graduate school. I was blissfully in love and anxious to become Mrs. Jarvis Bell."

"How nice," he grunted and clenched his teeth. "Your ex sounds like quite the charmer."

He was, and if I hadn't been so gullible and naive I wouldn't have fallen for his lies. Silencing her inner critic, she swallowed the lump at the back of her throat and willed herself not to cry. "Jarvis showed up unexpectedly at my dorm a few days before winter break, and I answered the door in a tank top and shorts. He looked mortified when he saw my scars and made up an excuse for why he had to leave."

"Thank God you found out the truth about him before it was too late."

Sharleen nodded, knew Emilio was right, but the memories of that day, and her ex-boyfriend's bitter rejection, still stung. "I was supposed to spend the holidays with Jarvis and his family in Maine, but he canceled my airline ticket the next day." Her voice cracked with emotion, so she faked an everything-is-okay smile for Emilio's benefit. "He said his parents changed their minds about meeting me and suggested we take a break for a while. Jarvis stopped calling and avoided me like the plague for the rest of the year."

"Baby, don't cry. He didn't deserve you, and you're better off without him."

Sharleen gave him a bewildered look. Touching her cheeks, she was shocked to discover they were wet. She wiped her face with the sleeve of her cardigan. "Unfortunately, Jarvis wasn't the only guy repulsed by my scars, and after being rejected repeatedly, I gave up on ever finding love. It doesn't exist, and I feel stupid for wasting my time searching for—"

Emilio put a finger to her lips and shook his head. "Don't talk like that. I think you're desirable and sexy and that will never change." He winked and added, "Not even when we're old and gray!"

Old and gray? You want a future with me? Seriously? Her head was spinning fast, out of control, and she couldn't stop shaking. Sharleen wanted to dance around the room to the song playing in her heart, but she told herself to relax. Despite her excitement, she sat silently, perfectly still, searching her heart for the courage to tell Emilio her *other* secret, the one no one knew but Jocelyn. She parted her lips and the truth fell out. "I'm a virgin."

An amused expression covered his face. "So am I."

"I've been on a lot of dates, but I've never met anyone I wanted to be intimate with. And I was too afraid they'd run for the hills after they saw my scars."

"You're serious." His eyes doubled in size, and his jaw dropped. "How is that possible? I see the way other guys look at you. They drool all over themselves!"

They do? Sharleen couldn't put her feelings into words, didn't even try.

"I'm speechless. I don't know what to say..." Emilio's cell phone rang, but he ignored it. When it started up again seconds later, he took it out of his pocket, turned it off and chucked it on the sofa love seat. "That's better. Now, where were we?"

"I don't mind if you answer your phone."

"I know, but I don't feel like talking to my sister."

"It could be important," she argued.

"Nothing is more important to me than being with you. This is our time alone together, and I don't want anyone to interrupt us."

Sharleen couldn't hide the smile that overwhelmed her lips. Forgetting the pain of her past, she entwined her fingers with his and giggled when he nipped at her earlobe.

"There's a common misconception that all men care about is sleeping with as many women as possible, but it's not true. At least not for me," he said. "I haven't had sex in years, and it suited me fine until I met you. Now it's *all* I can think about."

Sharleen was stunned, but she wore a blank expression on her face. Deciding to put all of her years of high school drama club to good use, she gasped and made her eyes big. "You've been celibate for years? How is that possible? I see the way other women look at you. They drool all over themselves!"

They laughed and held each other close, tighter than ever before. Nothing compared to being in his arms, to having his support.

"This isn't about sex. This is about us building a life together, and I want it all. Marriage, kids, family vacations to Disney World and romantic getaways to Monte Carlo."

Emilio spoke in a serious tone, but his gaze was filled with fire and desire. Sharleen ached for him, longed to be in his bed. She wanted him so bad she couldn't think of anything but making love to him. The problem was, Sharleen didn't know what to do. *Should I take charge? Would he like that? Will I?*

"You're not a one-in-a-million kind of girl, Sharleen. You're a once-in-a-lifetime kind of woman, and I'm ready to commit to you, mind, body and soul."

His words were obviously something he'd given serious thought to. Love flowed through her body, but she couldn't bring herself to say those three magic words. Sharleen felt as if she were dreaming, and she pinched herself to prove she was awake.

"I have one small request…"

I knew *this was too good to be true!*

"I'm tired of seeing you all covered up. Promise me you'll wear dresses and shorts and skirts from now on, and colors other than gray and black."

"I can't. I don't want anyone to see my scars."

"Everyone has something about themselves that they don't like. Even yours truly." Emilio pointed a finger at his temple. "Look, I'm cross-eyed!"

Sharleen burst out laughing and playfully swatted him on the shoulder. "Liar!"

"Courage isn't the absence of fear. It's the triumph over it," he said quietly. "Sharleen, put the past behind you and pursue your destiny with every fiber of your being."

Her mouth ajar, she stared at Emilio in stunned silence. Gathering herself, she gave him an incredulous look. "I can't believe it. You read Mrs. Fontaine's new book. But how? It was only released three days ago."

"I had no choice. You threatened to stop cooking for me if I didn't read it, and I can't live without your seafood gumbo!" Emilio cupped her chin in his hands and brushed his nose against hers, causing her to giggle. "I want you to wear the red Dior dress tonight. It was made for a woman with your curves, and the moment I saw it in the store window I thought of you."

You did? No way! That's so sweet!

"I want your outward appearance to reflect your inner beauty, so your Martha Stewart cardigans just aren't going to cut it anymore."

"But what if people stare at me?"

"Of course they're going to stare. You're a vibrant, exotic beauty. They can't help themselves." He kissed her softly on the lips. "And neither can I."

Chapter 15

"Oh, my gosh, look at the crowd!" Sharleen leaned forward in her seat and pointed through the back window of the limousine. The vehicle crawled to a stop at the entrance of the Miami Convention Center, but Emilio instructed the chauffeur to drive around to the rear of the building. Hundreds of fans, decked out in World Series Racing caps, T-shirts and leather bomber jackets were chanting his name. Their excitement consumed the air. "What a turnout. This is amazing. I've never seen anything like this."

"This is nothing compared to the Exotic Car Show in Barcelona. Ten thousand raucous fans show up every year, and they party in the streets until dawn!"

"Will you be traveling more now that you're Ferrari's spokesman?"

Emilio nodded. "I have to do TV and radio interviews and photo shoots, and I'll be required to attend industry events all over the world, especially in my native Italy."

"I love traveling, and I've always dreamed of going overseas, but I couldn't imagine spending fourteen hours on an airplane. That sounds like torture."

"Not if you're traveling in a private luxury jet. Trust me, it's the only way to travel."

"Snob!" she joked, with a laugh.

"I'm taking you to Monte Carlo for our honeymoon," he said. "You'll love it. I promise."

"Our honeymoon?" Sharleen laughed, as if it were the most outrageous thing she'd ever heard. But inside she was jumping for joy. The thought of being Mrs. Emilio Morretti made her heart swoon. For years, she'd pretended that she didn't need anyone, that she was content being single, but deep down she'd always wanted to be in a serious, committed relationship with someone who loved her unconditionally. And now the only man she wanted in her life was Emilio Morretti.

"Love is a risk worth taking, and I'm ready to take things to the next level. Are you?"

His words surprised her, so she took a few minutes to gather her thoughts. "Emilio, don't you think you're moving too fast? We haven't known each other long, and you just accepted a job that's going to take you around the world for months at a time."

Leaning over, he nuzzled his face against her cheek. "I want you to come with me."

Convinced he was joking, she laughed. But when she felt his body tense, she realized he was serious. Sharleen took great pride in having a successful career, owning her own home and having money in the bank, and she wouldn't walk away from everything that was important to her. "I just can't up and leave my job. I have responsibilities and clients who depend on me."

"You don't need to work."

"But I *want* to," Sharleen insisted, making a concerted effort not to raise her voice. Weeks ago, he'd joked about her quitting her job, but she'd assumed he was kidding and laughed it off. *Is that what Emilio wants? A docile woman at his beck and call who'll bend to his wishes, no matter how unreasonable they are?*

Her gaze searched his face, tried to figure out what he was thinking, how he was feeling. His expression was blank, but she sensed his disappointment, his frustration. Not wanting to argue with him, she gently caressed his fingers with her own. "My parents raised me to be independent, and I'll never be happy being a kept woman," she joked, hoping to lighten the mood. "I have hopes and dreams, just like you, and I plan to fulfill each and every one of them."

"Let me take care of you and give you the life you've always dreamed of."

"Emilio, I can take care of myself. I don't need you to baby me. I'm a grown woman."

"I don't want to date long-distance. I want you to travel with me."

"And I want to keep my career."

A scowl twisted his lips, and there was a hint of anger in his voice. "I can't believe we're arguing about this. Most women would kill to be able to stop working."

"Then I suggest you go find one of *those* women, because I refuse to be your puppet."

Emilio flinched, as if he'd been slapped. "We'll talk about this later."

What's there to talk about? I'm not quitting my job, and if you can't respect my decision then we'll never have a future together. Sharleen didn't realize the limousine had stopped until the back door opened, and sunshine flooded the car. She felt the wind on her face and took a deep breath of the sweet-smelling air to calm her nerves.

Emilio stepped out of the limo, helped Sharleen to her feet and draped an arm around her waist. He looked handsome in his red World Series Racing uniform, like the superstar athlete he was, and radiated a potent blend of sensuality and masculinity.

Out of the corner of her eye, Sharleen spotted a silver-haired man smoking at the back door of the convention center. She could feel the stranger looking at them, could feel the heat and intensity of his gaze. *Is he staring at Emilio or my scars?*

Sharleen thought back to that morning and smiled at the memory of their romantic breakfast. To please Emilio, she'd donned a flirty yellow dress and a pair of ankle-tie pumps. Butterflies had flooded her stomach as she'd entered the kitchen, but when he'd swept her up in his arms for a long, passionate kiss, her fears and insecurities had evaporated into thin air.

"Ready to wow the crowd?"

"I'm not the one with the rabid race-car fans," she told him. "No one will even notice me."

His gaze slid ever so slowly down her body and along her hips. "Oh, they'll notice all right." Emilio gave her a smile, one that made her forget about their argument minutes earlier. He lowered his mouth to her ear. "You take my breath away."

Sure I do, she thought, wishing he'd quit teasing her, but loving it nonetheless.

"Your legs look sensational in this dress." He licked his lips lasciviously, as if he wanted to devour her, and slid his hands down her back. "And so does your butt!"

"You are *such* a smooth talker. I bet your sexy one-liners drive your female fans wild."

"Confidence is sexy, so when I give you a compliment, just say thank you."

"Duly noted," she said.

A blonde, thinner than a lamppost, threw her arms around Emilio and kissed him on both cheeks. "You're here! I can't believe it!" she gushed. "You look incredible."

Emilio chuckled. "I've come a long way since I announced my retirement in 2012."

"I'd say. I almost didn't recognize you!"

"Love is an amazing thing." He looked at Sharleen and held her close to his side. He gazed at her with such warmth and affection her breath caught in her throat. "I haven't been this happy in years, and I owe it all to you."

Joy flooded her heart. Sharleen knew she was wearing an awestruck expression on her face, but she didn't care how foolish she looked. For years, she'd been afraid of intimacy, of letting anyone get too close, but now she wanted a future with Emilio, and she refused to let her doubts and insecurities get in her way. She loved him too much.

Emilio introduced her to the blonde, and Sharleen was surprised to discover the attractive stranger was a senior executive at Ferrari. The woman was her age, if not younger, and obviously had a huge crush on Emilio. *What else is new?* she thought, indulging in a wry smile. *He's a sexy piece of eye candy and more charismatic than a rock star!*

"Emilio, follow me." The blonde opened the back door of the convention center and waved him inside. "I have everything set up and ready to go on stage three."

The convention center was packed with car enthusiasts, members of the media and more scantily dressed women than a rap concert. Emilio stepped onto the raised booth, and the crowd exploded in cheers, whistles and fervent applause.

Sharleen was impressed by how kind he was to his fans. He kissed babies, posed for pictures and gave hugs. Women were coming at him from every side, but she could tell by his forced smile that he wasn't romantically interested in any of them.

Sharleen heard her cell phone ring inside her purse and knew from the ringtone that it was her boss. Panic drenched her skin. Did Mrs. Fontaine know that she was in Miami with Emilio? Was she calling to ream her out? Or worse, fire her? Putting the phone to her ear, she greeted her boss warmly, despite her thundering heartbeat. "Hello, Mrs. Fontaine. How are you?"

"Fine, thank you. Do you have a few minutes to talk?"

Frowning, she glanced down at her iPhone. Mrs. Fontaine sounded upset, as if she'd been crying, and her voice was softer than a whisper. "Yes, of course. Is everything okay?"

"I've made a decision about the VP position, and I would like to meet with you and Brad on Friday afternoon. I know you have a consultation, but I want everything in place before I leave for my book tour that evening."

"I understand, Mrs. Fontaine. Don't worry. I'll be there."

"Great. I look forward to seeing you—"

Sharleen heard muffled sounds and a gruff, male voice in the background, but it was Mrs. Fontaine's hostile tone that surprised her. "Jules, get the hell out or I'll call the cops!"

Click. The phone went dead. It seemed as if the rumors flying around the office were true. Mrs. Fontaine was having marital problems with her husband, Jules. Had she kicked him out of the house and changed the locks? Were they beginning divorce proceedings?

Casting her thoughts aside, she dropped her cell phone back inside her purse and turned to the stage. To her surprise, Emilio was staring at her. Their eyes met, and the corners of his mouth twisted into a bad-boy grin.

A tremor tore through her body, left her feeling delirious with need, and she shot him a playful wink. She'd never felt more comfortable in her skin, and Emilio was the reason why. It suddenly dawned on her what made him special. He appreciated her mind and praised her inner strength, not just her curves. He asked good questions, smart ones that made her search deep within, and she enjoyed their honest, thought-provoking discussions about life.

"You must be Sharleen," said a male voice, with a hint of an East Coast accent. Turning around, she regarded the attractive couple standing behind her, holding hands. Sharleen instantly recognized Nicco

Morretti from the pictures at Emilio's estate, but the photographs didn't do the restaurateur justice. He had eyes that twinkled with mischief, a head full of curly hair and a buff body. His wife, Jariah, was a tall, full-figured beauty with long, thick braids. Her orange off-the-shoulder sundress flattered her dark skin tone, and the tight fit showed off her baby bump.

"I'm Nicco, and this gorgeous woman is my wife, Jariah." Beaming with pride, he rested a hand on her stomach. "And this little one is Nicco Morretti Jr."

"It's a pleasure to meet you all."

"Welcome to the family," Nicco said, with a smile.

Sharleen laughed. It was impossible not to like Nicco—he was charming and outgoing, and she was touched by how he treated his wife. While they waited for Emilio, they chatted about the luxury cars on display and the record-breaking temperatures.

"I've been looking forward to meeting you for weeks, and now that I have, I understand why my cousin adores you," Nicco said. "So, when's the wedding?"

Sharleen felt her mouth dry and her cheeks burn with embarrassment.

"Nicco, leave her alone." Jariah wore a sympathetic smile. "You'll have to forgive my husband. We just came from Lamaze class, and the birthing videos always make him emotional."

"What can I say?" he said, throwing his hands in the air. "Love is a beautiful thing!"

The women laughed.

"Marriage definitely agrees with you, Nicco," Emilio said as he reached them. "I've never seen you look so good!"

Nicco hugged Emilio and introduced him to Jariah.

There were more hugs and kisses and plenty of laughs as the couples chatted.

"I hope you're not over here giving my girlfriend a hard time." Emilio glared at his cousin, but a broad grin was on his mouth. "It took me weeks to win her over, and I won't have you undoing all of my hard work."

Your girlfriend? God, I love the sound of that!

Sharleen thought her heart would burst with love when Emilio draped an arm around her waist and kissed her on the lips. He smiled knowingly at her, as if he had a trick up his sleeve, and affectionately stroked her neck and shoulders. His touch would never get old, would never fail to excite her, even if they were married for sixty years.

"Let's go eat." Emilio said. "Posing for pictures and signing autographs might look easy, but it's hard work!"

Three hours later, the couples were sitting outside on the wraparound deck at Nicco and Jariah's mansion, sipping cocktails and shooting the breeze. Too full to move, Sharleen sat back comfortably in her seat and crossed her legs. Dinner had been a five-course feast, and everything on the table—from the poached oysters to the Italian lamb—had been delicious.

"The big day is almost here," Emilio said. "Are you ready for the baby's arrival?"

Nicco shook his head. "Not yet. I still need a few more weeks to finish the nursery."

"And if the baby comes early?"

"Then I'm screwed!"

The men chuckled, and the jovial expression on Emilio's face made Sharleen laugh, too. His skin had browned in the sun, making him look even more attractive. It was obvious he was having a great time with his cousin, and Sharleen enjoyed seeing this playful, fun-loving side of him. He entertained them with stories from his childhood, told them about the first—and only—time he'd changed his nephew's diaper and spoke openly about how Lucca had changed his life.

"Having children will enrich your lives in ways you couldn't imagine."

"I wholeheartedly agree," Nicco said. "That's why I'd like to have five or six kids."

Jariah gestured to her stomach with a nod of her head. "Can I have this baby *first*, before you start pressuring me to have another one?"

The couple laughed and shared a kiss.

Sharleen glanced at Emilio, sensed that he was still thinking about his nephew and took his hand in hers. Their eyes met, and for a long moment they stared at each other, oblivious to the world around them.

"I found it!" Ava, Jariah's six-year-old daughter, burst through the French doors, waving a soccer ball in her hands. "I'm ready to show you my moves, Uncle Emilio!"

"Ava, honey, not now," Jariah said, hugging her daughter to her side. "Let your uncle finish his dessert. You can play soccer later."

Her face crumbled. "But I want to play now."

Emilio stood and smiled at the adorable girl with the short black curls. "Lead the way, Ava. I'm right behind you."

"Hey, wait for me!" Nicco jumped up, scooped his stepdaughter in his arms and nuzzled his chin against her cheek. "That's what you get for trying to leave me behind!"

She giggled uncontrollably. "Sorry, Dad, I didn't mean to."

"Next time you try to ditch me I'll bring out the Tickle Monster."

Ava gasped in horror, and everyone laughed.

Sharleen watched the trio set off for the field and giggled when Emilio blew her a kiss. Every time Emilio looked at her she felt as if her heart would burst with love.

"I think it's cute the way Emilio dotes on you," Jariah said, refilling their empty glasses with juice. "That's rare to see in this day and age."

"Tell me about it. The last guy I dated never referred to me as his girlfriend and he once introduced me to a colleague as his 'homie.' I almost died of embarrassment!"

"I hear you, girlfriend. I dated a lot of frogs before I met Nicco, so I'll never take him for granted. I thank God every day that we found each other."

Sharleen picked up her glass and tasted her drink. Her gaze strayed back to the field. Nothing was more attractive than a man playing with a child, and watching Emilio chase Ava around warmed her heart.

"Are you nervous about getting engaged?"

Sharleen choked on her mango punch. Mortified, she grabbed a napkin and covered her mouth as she coughed. "What makes you think Emilio and I are getting engaged?"

"I overheard the guys talking in the living room," she explained. "Emilio said he's ready to settle down, and that he'd like to be married by the end of the year."

"He said that? Really? But we've only known each other for a couple of months."

"When a man knows, he knows. And these Morretti men waste no time staking their claim."

"Is that what happened to you?"

"Yes, and I didn't even see it coming!" Jariah told her about the first time she met Nicco, about how she hated him on sight and her valiant efforts to resist his advances, especially after meeting his difficult, opinionated mother.

"But you can see how well *that* turned out," she quipped, rubbing her protruding stomach. "I never dreamed I'd get married and pregnant all in one year, but I wouldn't have it any other way. I'm glad I followed my heart. You should, too."

I want to, but I'm scared. What if he meets someone else? Someone beautiful and perfect and everything I'm not?

"Nicco told me you're the only woman Emilio's ever introduced him to—"

"No way! But he's dated tons of celebrities."

"That's true, but *you're* the one who captured his heart, and that's all that matters."

Her mind was reeling, spinning like a wheel. *Is Jariah right? Is he planning to propose? Is that why he brought me to Miami?*

"Can I give you some advice?"

Sharleen blinked and shook off her thoughts. "Yes, of course."

"Morretti men *always* get what they want, so don't bother playing hard to get. He'll sweep you off your feet, and before you know it, you'll be head over heels in love."

"Girl, please," Sharleen said with a laugh. "Tell me something I *don't* know!"

Chapter 16

"Baby, wake up. We're home." Emilio placed a hand on Sharleen's thigh, hoping she'd respond to his touch. She murmured in her sleep but didn't open her eyes. He wasn't surprised; they'd had a long day and he knew she was exhausted. They'd spent their last few hours in Miami strolling around South Beach, shopping for their friends and family at high-end boutiques.

After this weekend, he was more eager than ever to build a life with Sharleen. He caressed her cheeks with the back of his hand. What he loved most about Sharleen was her resilient spirit. She'd overcome insurmountable odds, but never lost her smile or her zest for life. She was good for him, someone kind and trustworthy who would do anything to make him happy, and he was excited about their future.

Emilio studied Sharleen, took his time admiring her

fit and fine physique. He didn't understand why a ridiculously beautiful woman would struggle with feelings of self-doubt and insecurity. More shocking still, she was a virgin. Emilio never would have guessed it, not in a million years. A puzzling thought crossed his mind. Did Antwan know Sharleen was a virgin? Was that why he wanted him to back off? Because he wanted to be her first?

Shaking his head, he told himself it didn't matter, that it wasn't important. Sharleen was his girlfriend now, and if Antwan wanted to keep their friendship, he'd leave her alone. It had happened all of a sudden, without him even realizing it, but he'd fallen hard for her.

Emilio nuzzled his face against hers and inhaled her scent. Her hair was styled just the way he liked, in loose, lush waves flowing down her back, and she was wearing one of the dresses he'd bought her. She was feminine and sexy, without revealing too much, and she carried herself in a graceful manner. Emilio was itching to make love to her, but he wouldn't pressure her. He'd wait until she was ready—

That could be six months from now, or a year? Can you handle being with her every day without crossing the line?

Emilio was pondering the question, when Sharleen opened her eyes and smiled sheepishly at him. "I drank too much wine on the flight, and it's all your fault. I told you one glass was enough, but you just wouldn't listen…"

"I like spoiling you. Is that a crime?"

Sharleen glanced outside the window. "I thought you were taking me home."

"I want you to spend the night."

She raised an eyebrow, and he did, too.

"Get your mind out of the gutter," he joked, faking a scowl. "I just want to hold you in my arms tonight. I might steal a couple kisses when you fall asleep, but that's it, I promise."

"Then I accept, but don't snore. I'm a light sleeper!"

Emilio slid out of his seat, came around to the passenger-side door and helped Sharleen out of his Escalade. He led her up the walkway and into his estate. "Are you hungry?" he asked, flipping on the lights in the foyer. "I could throw some steaks on the grill if you'd like."

"Sounds good to me," she said, flashing a cheeky smile. "I worked up *quite* an appetite making out with you in your private jet and I could use a good, hearty meal."

Emilio kissed her forehead. "I figured as much. Two T-bone steaks coming right up!"

Minutes later, he unlocked the French doors and stepped onto the deck. He turned on the grill, the fire pit and the stereo. Soft music played, and lights twinkled in the distance, creating a romantic mood. It was the perfect evening for stargazing, and Emilio was glad Sharleen was spending the night. Tomorrow was Memorial Day, and after his practice at the speedway, he was going to cook her an authentic Italian meal to celebrate his favorite American holiday.

"What do you want me to do?" Sharleen asked, sidling up beside him.

"Nothing. Just sit down and relax."

"But I want to help."

"Then get out of my way!" Chuckling good-naturedly,

he steered her over to the couch, dropped a kiss on her cheek and returned to the grill. While he cooked, Sharleen read online reviews to him about the car show. According to Sports.com, the event had been a hit, and everyone was still buzzing about his surprise appearance on Saturday afternoon.

"Listen to this," she said, in a loud, animated voice. "'Emilio Morretti wowed the crowd with his dashing good looks and dreamy accent, and long after he left the stage his fans were still screaming and cheering...'"

It was a challenge, but Emilio kept one eye on the steaks and the other on Sharleen. He couldn't go five minutes without looking at her, admiring her. Being with her was easy, as natural as breathing, and he knew he could never be happy with anyone else.

"Dinner is served!" Emilio put the food on the table and sat down beside Sharleen on the couch. As they ate, they talked about their weekend in Miami, the car show and how much fun they'd had last night at Nicco and Jariah's estate. They moved comfortably from one subject to the next, and when Emilio glanced at his watch he was shocked to discover it was midnight. "I can't believe we've been sitting here for three hours," he said. "We should turn in. I have practice in the morning, and you have to be at the office by noon."

"Can we stay out here a little bit longer? I'm not tired, and I'm having a great time."

Emilio couldn't take his eyes off of her, and the sound of her voice turned him on. She had the most amazing personality, and her smile was a thing of beauty. He wanted to kiss her, to stroke and caress her shapely body, but feared that if he did he wouldn't be able to stop.

"I love this song." Sharleen snapped her fingers and swayed to the beat of the music. "Mariah Carey is my favorite singer, and I listened to this song so much my freshman year that my roommate confiscated the CD!"

"Dance with me." Emilio swept her up in his arms and spun her around the deck. They danced in the moonlight, talking and laughing. "I've given a lot of thought to what you said on Saturday, and I've decided not to sign with Ferrari."

"But they're offering you millions of dollars and the opportunity to resurrect your career."

"I'll compete in the All-Star race, but I won't be their celebrity spokesman. I want to be with you, not thousands of miles away doing interviews and photo shoots."

She stared at him in amazement, as if she didn't understand what he was saying. "Emilio, are you sure about this? You're turning down a lot of money."

"I have everything a man could want, and all I need now is the right woman to complete the picture. And that's you."

"I feel the same way," she said, tenderly stroking the back of his head. "When we're together I'm happier than I've ever been."

"I was hoping you'd say that." Emilio tightened his hold around her waist, held her close. "I want to open the Lucca Morretti Recreation Center next year, but I can't do it without you. You're full of great ideas, and you're one of the smartest people I know."

"Now I *really* want you!"

Her kiss blindsided him. Sharleen pressed her body against his and crushed her lips to his mouth. She kissed him so hard, with such passion and intensity, he stumbled into one of the potted plants. She tasted sweet, of wine, and her hands felt warm against his skin.

Emilio didn't know what had gotten into Sharleen, but he liked it—a lot. This was not what he was expecting when he'd brought her home from the airport, and her aggressive, take-charge attitude blew his mind. Turned on, he couldn't think of anything but making love to her.

Sharleen parted her lips slightly, to let him in, and he eagerly accepted the invitation. She sucked his tongue into her mouth, licked it as if it were covered in chocolate. Emilio told himself to calm down, but it was hard to control his desires when she was grinding her hips against his crotch. "Take me upstairs to your bedroom."

"Do you want me to draw you a bath?"

"No, I want you to make love to me."

She gave him *the look*, and his mouth dried. Emilio stood motionless, paralyzed. *Did she just say what I think she did?* Determined to do the right thing, he dropped his hands to his sides and took a step back. "I respect your decision to wait—"

"I don't want to wait. I've given this a lot of thought, and I want you to be my first."

His lust spiked. She slowly licked his ear with her tongue. A groan fell out of his mouth. Then another one. His heart was thumping wildly in his chest, and his mind was jumping from one explicit thought to the next. Emilio couldn't concentrate, and he struggled to reclaim his voice.

"Don't you want to make love to your very sexy, very horny life coach?"

You have no idea. Emilio wanted to rip off her dress,

bend her over the couch and bury himself so deep inside her they became one. But he shook his head and held her at arm's length. "I think you've had too much to drink."

"And I think you're scared I'm going to rock your world."

Her bold declaration stunned him, blew his mind. Sharleen was the sexiest virgin he'd ever met, and by far the most beautiful, but he wouldn't take advantage of her. Not tonight, not ever. Tomorrow, she'd thank him for ignoring her sexual advances and probably have a good laugh about her antics.

"I'm wearing red lace panties. Do you want to see them?"

Hell yeah! His face must have betrayed his desire, because Sharleen took his hand and led him back into the house and up the staircase. His second-floor master suite was spacious, filled with luxurious furnishings and framed oil paintings from Italy.

"This is quite the bachelor pad," Sharleen said, glancing around. "You must entertain in here a lot."

"No, this is my private sanctuary, and completely off-limits to guests." He smiled. "Except you, of course. You can come in here anytime you want."

She walked over to the floor-to-ceiling window overlooking the car-shaped pool and pulled back the burgundy silk drapes. "Wow, what an amazing view."

"It pales in comparison to your beauty."

Emilio watched her as she fiddled with her fingers and knew coming upstairs to his suite had been a mistake. He longed to make love to her, but tonight wasn't the night. Spending time with her the past few weeks had made him realize how shallow his previous relationships had been, and Emilio was determined to build a long, lasting relationship with Sharleen. Not one based solely on sex.

"This is all new to me," she said, with a shy smile. "What happens now?"

"Sharleen, we don't have to do this. There's no rush."

Her face fell. "You don't want me—"

"Of course I do. You're sexy and vivacious and beautiful." To prove it, he pulled her into his arms for a kiss. He didn't want to come on too strong, but one kiss wasn't enough. He loved her with his mouth, feasted on her lips until his body ached for her. Emilio was weak, desperate for her, and each slow, sensuous kiss intensified his hunger, his need.

Emilio broke off the kiss and cupped her chin in his hands. He forced her to look at him. "I want you more than I've ever wanted anyone, but I don't want you to do something you'll regret in the morning. We can wait."

"Don't you think we've waited long enough?"

"We have the rest of our lives to make love. What's a few more months?"

Sharleen grazed her lips against his ear and whispered, "But I want you *now.*"

The sound of her throaty, sultry voice made his head spin. He'd never seen her like this and wondered what had gotten into her. Her touch was passionate, urgent, her words a desperate plea. She knew what he needed, what his body was craving, and she was giving it to him. Emilio struggled to control himself, felt as if his mind and flesh were at odds. He hadn't been intimate with anyone in years and was secretly nervous about making love to Sharleen. Would he please her? Would they be sexually compatible?

"Emilio, kiss me."

He did. Over and over again, until she was breathless. His heartbeat pounded in his ears, roared like thunder, and his erection was harder than steel. He couldn't fight his feelings anymore, wasn't strong enough to resist her. They stumbled around the room kissing and caressing each other, and they laughed when the cordless phone fell off the side table and crashed to the floor. Emilio stroked her body with loving tenderness, took his time pleasing her. They kissed for what felt like hours, but it wasn't enough. He needed more. He had to have her. Now. Before he lost the battle with his flesh and exploded inside his jeans.

"Your clothes are in my way," he said. "Turn around so I can unzip your dress."

"Not until you close the drapes."

Emilio saw the fear in her eyes, the trepidation, and hugged her to his chest. To reassure her, he tenderly stroked her hair, neck and shoulders. "Please don't deny me the pleasure of seeing you naked. I think you're gorgeous, and I want to see every inch of your body."

Her face brightened, glowed with happiness.

"You're so beautiful it blows my mind," he whispered, nibbling on her earlobe. "But you're more than just a pretty face, Sharleen. You're the total package, and don't you forget it."

He must have said the right thing, must have put her doubts to rest, because she sighed dreamily, as if she was overcome with love, and kissed him hard on the lips. Emilio took his time undressing her, savored the moment. He unzipped her dress, let it fall to the floor and admired her curvy shape for several seconds. Sharleen was perfection. Big, beautiful breasts, wide hips, silky brown legs he could almost feel wrapped around his waist and a tight ass.

"You're staring."

"Of course I am. You're stunning." He cupped her chin in his hand and forced her to meet his gaze. "When I look at you, I don't see scars or imperfections. I see a strong, tenacious young woman who beat the odds and built a great life for herself. You're beautiful, inside and out, and I want you more than I've ever wanted anyone."

A grin warmed her mouth. Taking his hands in her own, she used them to stroke her nipples. His pulse sped up, beat in double time, and his erection grew thicker, wider.

Feeling as if he was losing control, he cautioned himself to slow down. This was Sharleen's first time, and he wanted to make it a night she'd never forget. With that thought in mind, he scooped her up, carried her across the room and laid her down on his satin-draped bed.

Emilio kicked off his shoes and took off his clothes. He dug around in his dresser, found a box of MAGNUM condoms and sighed in relief. He covered his erection and gathered Sharleen in his arms.

He cupped her breasts, sucked her nipples into his mouth, teased and tickled the dark, erect buds with his tongue. His only concern was pleasing her, fulfilling her every desire, every unspoken wish. He parted the lips between her legs and slid a finger inside her sex. Emilio was surprised—and pleased—to discover she was wet, ready. He swirled his fingers around, slid them in and out, back and forth. "Do you like that? Does that feel good?"

The word *amazing* fell out of her mouth in a gush.

Hearing her moans and groans thrilled him. She rode his fingers, rocked her hips hard against them. Sharleen was losing it, coming undone, and Emilio loved watching every erotic minute of it.

Seizing his shaft in her hands as if she owned it, she brushed it against her sex, like an artist with a paintbrush. Each flick of his erection against her sex pushed him to the brink. She clutched his shoulders, held on to him for dear life.

An orgasm seized her body, caused her to shake so violently the headboard banged against the wall. Another one, longer and more powerful, followed on the heels of the first. She swiveled her hips in a slow, hypnotic rhythm, one that made him feel as if he was going to explode. Emilio had never seen anything like it, never experienced such passion, and her excitement was the ultimate turn-on.

Moments later, her breathing slowed, her tremors subsided, and she opened her eyes.

"This is torture. I can't take this anymore. I need to be inside you."

Her eyes were wide, her face the picture of innocence, but she was wearing a cheeky smile. "Baby, are you sure? I don't want you to do anything you're not comfortable with."

Emilio grinned, couldn't help it. She was teasing him, ribbing him about what he'd said earlier, but he didn't mind. Not this time, not when they were having fun together.

Her gaze was seductive, so damned hypnotic Emilio

felt as if he was under her spell. She whispered dirty words in his ear, eagerly stroked his package, didn't hold back. It was obvious she wanted him, just as much as he wanted her, and the realization made him feel like the luckiest man on earth.

He guided his erection between her legs and eased the tip inside her sex. She was tight and so damned wet that Emilio feared he'd climax right away. Adrenaline pumped through his veins, stole his breath, and every coherent thought left his mind. Being inside Sharleen was the best feeling in the world. He wanted to own her, possess her, and brand her with his body so no one else could. *And I will, one stroke at a time.*

They shared a deep kiss fraught with lust and desire. He thrust his erection inside her, again and again, parted her legs wide to deepen his penetration. Their lovemaking was intense, more exciting than doing three hundred miles an hour around the track in his custom-made Ferrari race car. Emilio lowered his mouth for a kiss and froze when he saw tears in her eyes. "Did I hurt you?"

Sharleen sniffed and shook her head, but he wasn't convinced.

"These are tears of joy," she said softly. "I never dreamed I could be this happy."

"Baby, are you sure? I can stop if you're in pain."

"Oh, no, you don't. We're *just* getting started." She traced her finger around his nipple, stroked it, teased it, sucked it hungrily into her mouth. "Emilio, you're amazing. I love the way you make me feel. Please don't stop…"

"Since you asked so nicely…" He kissed her mouth. Her lips tasted sweet, warm and soft against his. Emilio wrapped her up in his arms, held her so close to his chest he could feel her heart pounding. "You were definitely worth the wait."

She locked her arms around his neck and nibbled on his lower lip. "I can honestly say you're the best lover I've *ever* had."

The sound of her girlish laugh made him chuckle, too.

"I love you so much that it scares the hell out of me." Emilio cupped her face in his hands and confessed what he'd been holding inside for months. "I don't know what I'd ever do if I lost you."

"You never have to worry about losing me because I'm not going anywhere. My heart is yours, and always will be." Sharleen placed soft, light kisses on his cheeks, along his jawline and down his neck. "I don't want anyone else, Emilio. Just you."

Shock waves coursed through his body, stealing his voice. He increased his pace, thrust his erection deeper inside her sex. Emilio felt his erection swell and released a deep, guttural groan. Sharleen clamped her legs around his thighs and kissed him passionately. The tingling sensation in his feet shot up his legs, zigzagged along his spine and exploded inside his shaft. Clutching her hips, he furiously pumped. His climax was so powerful, so intense, Emilio felt as if he'd been struck by a bolt of lightning.

And did it ever feel good.

Chapter 17

Sharleen stared at the high-tech Swiss coffee machine, annoyed that she couldn't figure out how to use it. She searched the kitchen drawers for the instruction manual, but couldn't find it anywhere. Everything was ready—the scrambled eggs, the Belgian waffles, the hash-brown frittatas—and all she needed now was a cup of espresso to complete Emilio's breakfast. "I can make a three-course meal with my eyes closed, but I can't get this stupid thing to work," she grumbled. "Go figure!"

She heard her ringtone, knew it was Jocelyn calling to check up on her, but she continued fiddling with the fancy machine. She'd call her girlfriend later, after Emilio left for practice, and fill her in on her weekend in Miami and her romantic night. Sharleen felt as if she were floating, gliding on air, and wondered if her feet would ever touch the ground. *Jocelyn's going to flip when I tell her I'm not a virgin anymore. I can hardly believe it myself!*

Sharleen picked up the plates, padded across the kitchen and put them on the glass table. She felt a dull ache in her forearms and decided a massage at her favorite spa that evening was definitely in order. Her body was sore, tender all over, but she wouldn't trade making love to Emilio for anything in the world. He was a patient, sensitive lover, who put her needs above his own. After making love that morning for the second time, he'd carried her into the bathroom and given her a bath in his Jacuzzi tub. Emilio was in his office now, on a video conference call with Ferrari executives, and since Sharleen wanted to have everything ready by the time he came downstairs for breakfast, she hustled back over to the stove and flipped the pancakes.

"My, my, my, what do we have here?"

Startled, the spatula fell from Sharleen's hands. She turned to face the female voice. A brunette, decked out in Louis Vuitton from head to toe, was standing beside the stainless-steel fridge, glaring at her. Sharleen recognized Emilio's sister from the family portrait hanging in the foyer and marveled at how striking the former model was.

Gathering her bearings, she turned off the stove, scooped up the spatula and dropped it into the sink. Sharleen inwardly chastised herself for leaving the master bedroom in Emilio's undershirt and shorts. Just because his staff had the day off work didn't mean they had the house to themselves. *Talk about an awkward first meeting,* Sharleen thought, combing her fingers through the ends of her disheveled hair. *Why didn't Emilio tell me his sister was joining us for breakfast?*

Taking shelter behind the breakfast bar, she crossed her arms to hide her braless state and forced a smile. "You must be Francesca," she said brightly, refusing to let her nerves get the best of her. "It's a pleasure to finally meet you."

"The feeling isn't mutual, so get out."

Sharleen was stunned by her rudeness, but she wisely bit her tongue. She knew Francesca's story and sympathized with her, but losing a child didn't give her the right to be disrespectful. Because she loved Emilio, she'd be nice; but if his sister didn't kill the attitude they were definitely going to have a problem.

"Okay...well. Breakfast is ready. Are you joining us?"

Francesca scoffed and rolled her eyes. "As if. Carbs are, like, *so* fattening."

"If you change your mind there's plenty, so feel free to help yourself."

"How long has this been going on?" she asked, dumping her handbag on the kitchen counter. "And do you screw all of your male clients, or just the rich ones?"

Pity tempered her anger, made her swallow the stinging retort on the tip of her tongue. Francesca was upset, lashing out at her because Emilio had cut her off financially, but Sharleen refused to be her human punching bag. "It's obvious you're upset, so I'll go get Emilio so the two of you can talk about what's bothering you."

"My issue is with you, bitch, not my brother."

The insult and her icy tone confused Sharleen. On the outside, Sharleen was the picture of calm, but her temples were throbbing in pain, and her heart was pounding violently. She remained silent, and although she was annoyed with Francesca for swearing at her, she didn't lash back.

"I'm not going to stand by and watch you play my brother for a fool."

"This conversation is over," she said calmly, in a tone that disguised her frustration. "My relationship with Emilio is none of your business, and furthermore, we don't need your permission to date."

"Emilio will never marry you, so you might as well quit while you're ahead." Scowling, her lips pinched with distaste, Francesca tapped her foot impatiently on the ground. "You're just something cute and young to play with until he finds the right woman."

Maybe instead of throwing stones, you should examine your own life, you spoiled brat! Not trusting herself to speak, for fear she'd lose her temper, Sharleen swiped her cell phone off the counter and strode past Francesca.

"Does Emilio know about your hefty five-figure bonus?"

Her body went cold, rigid with shock, and she stopped dead in her tracks.

"That's right. I know all about the money, and I have the proof right here…"

Panic welled inside her chest, caused sweat to drench her skin. Sharleen heard papers ruffle and knew Francesca had evidence to back up her claim. Guilt gnawed at her conscience. *I should have ripped up the check instead of giving it to Jocelyn, but what was I supposed to do? She's out of work, and she desperately needed the money!*

Telling herself not to panic, she turned and faced Francesca. The brunette was clutching a piece of paper in her right hand and pointing at her with the other. She stared her down, like a prizefighter consumed with rage, her eyes blazing with anger.

"Antwan paid you ten thousand dollars to seduce my brother, and I can prove it," she said, her tone so confident, she sounded like a state prosecutor who knew every angle of her case. "Antwan wanted Emilio to come out of retirement, and he used *you* to make it happen."

Sharleen opened her mouth to deny the accusation, but she couldn't get the words out. The truth got stuck in her throat, and her heart was beating so hard she couldn't think.

"Is it true?"

Her stomach pitched to the floor when she heard Emilio's voice. She glanced over her shoulder, saw him standing directly behind her and felt the baby-fine hairs on the back of her neck shoot up. He stared at her intently, as if they were strangers, and folded his arms rigidly across his chest.

The room darkened, and the air grew thick with tension.

"Is it true?" he repeated, raising his voice. "Were you paid to seduce me?"

Sharleen felt as if she were drowning, as if someone were holding her head under water. She struggled to catch her breath. She didn't have it in her to lie—not to Emilio, not after everything he'd done for her—so she opened her mouth and forced her lips to move. "I—I apologize for not telling you about the bonus, but it's not what you think."

"Of course it is!" Francesca raged, throwing her hands up in the air. "You're nothing but a whore, and my brother can do better than you. All you care about is his money—"

"Francesca, that's enough. Go wait for me in the living room."

"And leave you here with her? No way. I'm not going anywhere," she said, adamantly shaking her head. "She's trouble with a capital *T*, and I don't trust her."

Ignoring the dig, Sharleen approached Emilio, determined to plead her case. "Please, let me explain." She touched his forearm to remind him of the love they shared and forced him to meet her gaze. "Antwan sent me a check in the mail last week, but I signed it over to my best friend so she could use it to pay her mom's medical bills."

"Likely story," Francesca grumbled, her tone dripping with sarcasm. "How noble of you. You're a modern-day Mother Teresa."

"I have no reason to lie. It's the truth."

"Sure it is. Next you'll be telling us you didn't hire a photographer to take pictures of you guys and leak the photographs online."

Emilio frowned and glanced at his sister. "What are you talking about?"

"I called you yesterday to give you a heads-up, but you never answered your phone." Francesca took her iPhone out of her purse and tapped the screen. "The press is having a field day with the pictures of you guys kissing on your motorcycle at Centennial Olympic Park…"

Sharleen hung her head and pressed her eyes shut. *This can't be happening. Not today.* Feeling herself getting emotional, she bit the inside of her cheek to keep the tears at bay. She'd worked hard to keep their relationship secret, hadn't even told her closest friends. And wondered how the media attention would affect her career.

"Did you have anything to do with this?" His eyes were dark, filled with anger, and he was shouting his words. "Did you leak these pictures to advance your career? Is that what this is about?"

Stunned, Sharleen dropped her hands to her sides and stepped away from Emilio. She felt a sharp, sudden pain in her chest and a cold chill zip down her spine. Her heart shattered into a million pieces, crumbled like rubble. Telling herself not to panic, she willed herself to keep it together despite the weight of her sadness. "No, of course not. I had nothing to do with it."

"The things you said last night…" He paused to clear his throat. "Were you telling the truth? Or just doing your job?"

His words were a vicious blow, as painful as a slap in the face. Her back was against the wall, and there was no way out. She stood there, mute, willing herself to speak, to defend her good name, but her lips wouldn't work.

A long painful silence followed, and Sharleen knew, deep down, that Emilio didn't believe her. *Doesn't he know that I'm different? That I'm not like his relatives and ex-lovers who betrayed him in the past? That I'd never do anything to hurt him? Didn't last night mean anything to him?*

Her vision blurred with tears.

"You should go." His voice broke, but he quickly recovered. "I need to be alone."

"I understand." It was a lie, but she decided not to argue. Sharleen was afraid if she challenged him, he'd be gone, out of her life forever. And she couldn't risk losing him. Not now. Not after everything they'd been through. Emilio made her feel strong and empowered, as if she could do anything she put her mind to, and she wanted to spend the rest of her life with him. Her female intuition told her Francesca had something to do with the photographs, but since she didn't have any proof, Sharleen kept her suspicions to herself.

Pushing her hurt aside, she smiled through her tears and nodded her head. "I'll wait for you upstairs in the master bedroom, and we can talk whenever you're ready—"

"No, I think it's better you leave."

But I don't want to go home! I want to stay here with you!

"I'll ask one of the groundskeepers to drive you back to the city."

An awkward silence descended over the kitchen. It lasted so long Sharleen thought it would never end. With each passing second her anxiety grew, and she worried about their future together as a couple. Emilio wouldn't look at her, refused to make eye contact, and his face was twitching as if he was about to sneeze. "I'll call you."

Hope surged through her veins. "When?"

"I don't know." Emilio turned around and strode out through the back door.

Sharleen peered out of the kitchen window, tracking his movements as the distance between them grew. Her thoughts returned to last night, and her heart ached when she remembered how they'd talked and kissed and danced outside on the deck. Emilio made her feel whole, more comfortable and confident than she'd ever been. He was the only man for her, and—

"Didn't you hear what my brother said?" Francesca smiled in satisfaction and pointed down the hallway. "Goodbye and good riddance!"

Chapter 18

Every time Sharleen's cell phone rang, butterflies swarmed her stomach. But when she realized it was another pesky telemarketer calling, and not Emilio, her spirits fell. *Why hasn't he called? Doesn't he miss me? Doesn't he want to work things out?* She hadn't seen or heard from him since she left his estate on Memorial Day, and she wasn't sure if she'd ever see him again. For the past four days, guilt had been her constant companion. Sharleen regretted not telling Emilio about the bonus, but she'd feared that if she'd told him the truth he would have broken up with her. *Some good that did me,* she thought miserably. *He found out and dumped me anyway.*

Her gaze strayed to her wall calendar, zeroed in on the date. They hadn't spoken in four days, but it felt like months since she'd heard his voice or seen his face.

Emilio had promised to call but hadn't. She'd sent him text messages, emails and even tropical flowers from his favorite florist shop, but he still hadn't reached out to her. A troubling thought came to mind, one that made her heart throb in pain. *Has Emilio found someone else? Is that why he hasn't called? Because he's forgotten all about me?*

Driven by fear, Sharleen picked up her desk phone and punched in his cell number. The call went straight to voice mail, but she didn't hang up. "Hey, it's me again." She paused, took a deep breath to calm her nerves and wiped her damp palms along the side of her sleeveless dress. This was the third message she'd left for Emilio today, and this time she was determined to be concise, not emotional and upset. "I haven't heard from you since Monday, and I just wanted to see how you're doing. Please call me when you get a chance."

Sharleen lowered the phone, remembered something else she wanted to say and put it back to her ear. "I miss you, Emilio. I know you think the worst of me right now, but I want you to know that I love you and always will, no matter what."

Hanging up the phone, she dropped her face in her hands and released a deep sigh. At the office, she put on a brave face, acted as if everything was okay, but inside she was an emotional wreck. She wasn't eating much, had skipped her Stiletto Aerobics three days in a row and hadn't had a good night's sleep since she'd left Emilio's estate. Last night, she'd dreamed Francesca was chasing her around his kitchen with a butter knife, and she'd woken up drenched in sweat.

Determined not to spend the entire day fretting about her problems, she logged on to her computer, typed in her password and opened her file on Rashad J. The R&B superstar was a handful, but rereading her session notes was the perfect distraction. Hard at work, despite the thoughts of Emilio crowding her mind, she didn't hear Antwan enter her office and yelped when he touched her shoulder. "Don't sneak up on me like that. You scared me half to death," she said, resting a hand on her pounding, thundering chest. "What are you doing here?"

"I heard about your showdown with Francesca on Monday and thought you might need to see a friendly face. And since I was in the neighborhood, I decided to drop by."

Sharleen evaded his gaze by rearranging the pictures on her desk. "That was very sweet of you, but you shouldn't have wasted your time. I'm fine."

"Are you mad at me?"

"Did you give Francesca a copy of the check you mailed me?"

"No, of course not," he said, shaking his head. "I hired her to help me around the office for a few weeks, but when I found out she was snooping through my personal files, I fired her."

Antwan leaned against her desk and gave her a slow appraising glance. "In all the years we've been friends I've never seen you in a dress." He winked and grinned like a leprechaun who'd found a pot of gold. "You look amazing, Sharleen. Love *definitely* agrees with you."

Sharleen started to dismiss his compliment with a wave of her hand, then remembered what Emilio had said to her last week at the Exotic Car Show and nodded her thanks.

"Do you want to talk about what happened?"

She asked the question at the forefront of her mind. "How is Emilio doing?"

Antwan pointed at her desk phone. "Why don't you call him and find out?"

"I tried, but he won't take my calls."

"So, that's it? You're just going to throw in the towel?"

You don't understand. Being rejected hurts, and I'm scared of putting myself out there—

"Emilio's crazy about you, so hurry over to his estate before he leaves for Milan."

Sharleen shot straight up in her chair. "How long will he be gone for?"

"He's attending the Classic Car Show in Milan this weekend, then spending some time with his friends and family. He'll be back in town a couple days before the All-Star Race."

Her head spun, and her heart thumped. *He'll be gone for the entire summer? But doesn't he know I'll miss him terribly? Does he even care?*

"I can't go to his house. What if he won't talk to me? Or walks out on me again?"

"He won't. Emilio loves you, and he's miserable without you."

"Then why hasn't he returned any of my calls? Why hasn't he reached out to me?"

"Because he feels guilty," Antwan explained, wearing a thoughtful expression on his face. "Emilio knows he messed up, but he's scared to make the first move. He's worried you'll reject him."

I'm so confused. I don't know what to think.

"Give some serious thought to what I said." Antwan

kissed her on the cheek and stood. "You don't have much time, though. Emilio leaves for Milan at six o'clock."

Sharleen gasped. "Tonight? And you're just telling me now? Some friend you are!"

Antwan chuckled and slipped on his sunglasses. "How are things going with Rashad J?"

"Terrible. He's spoiled and cocky, and he treats everyone around him like crap."

"I know, that's why I advised Urban Beats Records to hire you. If you can't save the Bedroom Maestro from himself, no one can."

For the first time that day, Sharleen laughed. But when Antwan left her office seconds later, the heaviness in her chest returned. The only place she felt safe and loved was with Emilio, and she longed to be back in his arms. She thought about their romantic weekend in Miami, the night they'd made love, their whispered promises and declarations. They were more than just lovers—they were best friends, and Sharleen missed having him to talk to. He was warm and affectionate, always made her feel good about herself and never failed to make her laugh. Emilio was the kind of man a woman didn't forget, and Sharleen feared she never would.

"I want you both to know I thought long and hard about this decision." Mrs. Fontaine clasped her hands on her desk and glanced from Brad to Sharleen. "After serious deliberation, I decided to choose the person I feel embodies all of the traits and characteristics I'm looking for in a vice president."

Sharleen nodded, as if she were listening, but her thoughts were a million miles away. This meeting was just a formality, and the only reason she'd come to her boss's office that afternoon was because Mrs. Fontaine had personally summoned her. On Monday, as she was leaving Emilio's estate, her boss had called her cell phone and interrogated her like a homicide detective. Their thirty-minute conversation had been tense, plagued with sighs and long bouts of silence, and when the call ended, Sharleen knew there was no way in hell she was getting the VP job. But she had bigger problems to deal with than losing the promotion to Brad. What was she going to do about Emilio? Should she cut her losses and move on or drive to his estate and force him to talk to her?

"Congratulations, Ms. Nichols. I hope you make the most of this life-changing opportunity…"

Sharleen blinked and surfaced from her thoughts. "I'm the new vice president of Pathways Center?"

Mrs. Fontaine laughed. "Yes, you are. You're the perfect person for the job, and I'm thrilled you're going to be my right hand."

"This is bullshit! *I* deserve to be VP." Brad jabbed a finger at his chest. "I've been at this center for nine years, and no one works harder than I do."

"Brad, calm down," Mrs. Fontaine said. "You're yelling."

"Sharleen can't be vice president," he continued, his voice deafening. "She's screwing her clients for money, and God knows what else."

"That's a lie, and you know it!" Sharleen met his gaze, refused to back down. Brad was a jerk, nothing more than a bully in an Armani suit, and she'd had enough of his self-righteous behavior. "You have no right to judge me. You're an embarrassment to this profession, and you give life coaches everywhere a bad name."

Brad laughed off her comment. "My clients would beg to differ."

Yeah, probably because you're blackmailing them!

"Check out FameAndFortune.com," he said, pointing at Mrs. Fontaine's computer. "There are pictures of Sharleen and Emilio Morretti all over the internet. Kissing in front of her house, making out in his Escalade, draped all over each other in the airport VIP lounge…"

Sharleen frowned and cocked her head to the side. *What's Brad talking about? There were no pictures of me and Emilio at the airport.* Unless… Realization dawned, and her eyes widened in surprise. The truth was staring her right in the face. She didn't want to believe it, but it was Brad—not Francesca—who'd set her up to fall. "You've been spying on me!" she raged, anger pounding furiously through her veins. All the pieces of the jigsaw puzzle fell into place, and the devilish grin on Brad's face confirmed her suspicions. "*You* took those pictures and sold them to humiliate me!"

"You humiliated *yourself*, toots, so don't blame me for your problems."

Mrs. Fontaine raised a hand to silence them, then addressed Brad seconds later. "I value the contributions you've made to Pathways, and I admire your drive and tenacity, but my decision is final. If you'd like to discuss this matter further, I can meet with you when I return from my book tour next—"

"Go home, save your marriage and forget about that stupid book tour," Brad snapped, rudely cutting her off. "I can run the center in your absence."

"Excuse me?" Mrs. Fontaine narrowed her eyes and gripped the arms of her leather chair.

"Jules is running around with other women, and you're too busy promoting your new book to notice." Brad shook his head as if he were admonishing a child. "He practically lives at the strip club. In fact, he's at Club Onyx so much the owner gave him his own parking spot!"

Mrs. Fontaine stood and pointed at the door. "Brad, that's enough. Please leave."

"With pleasure, and I'll be taking my celebrity contacts with me."

Sharleen watched him swagger out of the office and was relieved to see him go. He was a loose cannon, and the center was better off without him. At least the pictures of Jocelyn—and the other women he'd been blackmailing—had been destroyed when he spilled coffee on his iPhone. But Sharleen wondered if Brad had any other tricks up his sleeve. He was out for revenge, but she wasn't going down without a fight.

"I'm sorry Brad lashed out at you, but he's going through a difficult time right now."

"Yes, I can imagine. Having to program his new iPhone must be *extremely* stressful."

Mrs. Fontaine gestured to the chair in front of her desk. Sharleen didn't want to hear about what a great life coach Brad was, or about all the big names he'd signed over the years, but she sat down and crossed her legs. She was curious about the accusations Brad had made about Mrs. Fontaine's husband, Jules, but didn't dare ask the questions in her mind. It was none of her business, and she didn't want to upset her boss.

"Brad's wife walked out on him last year and took

their three young sons with her. He hasn't seen his boys in months, and it's killing him inside. He's angry at the world right now, and he's taking his frustration out on everyone around him, especially women. I'm not making excuses for his behavior, but I do empathize with him."

"I had no idea Brad was having personal problems, or that he had a wife and kids, but there's no excuse for his behavior."

"You're right, and I'm working with the HR department to investigate the claims that have been brought to my attention," she explained. "I'm disappointed with the choices Brad's made, but he's worked at Pathways since day one, and I feel compelled to help him find his children. They're sweet little boys who need their father."

Though she was angry at Brad for harassing Jocelyn, and spying on her, Sharleen understood why Mrs. Fontaine wanted to help him.

"By any chance, have you met Emilio's brother Immanuel Morretti?"

"No, I haven't," Sharleen said. "They've been estranged from each other for years. Why?"

"Apparently, he's one of the best private investigators in the business, and his agency, Mastermind Operations, recently opened offices in Atlanta. You're fooling around with his kid brother, so I figured you could give me some additional information on him."

Sharleen dropped her gaze to her lap. She couldn't talk about Emilio without tearing up, and she knew if she didn't change the subject she'd burst into tears. "Why did you give me the VP position?" she asked, her curiosity getting the best of her. "What was the deciding factor?"

"You did something no one else has ever done, and I was impressed with your ingenuity."

Sharleen thought for a moment, tried to figure out what her boss was referring to, but came up empty. "What did I do?"

"You orchestrated the perfect publicity stunt, and now my phone is ringing off the hook!"

It wasn't a publicity stunt. I love Emilio with all my heart, and I want to marry him.

"I have ten thousand new Twitter followers, and on-line searches for Pathways Center have surged by one hundred percent!" Her eyes were bright with excitement. "I told you to create more buzz and attract more clients, and you delivered big-time."

"My feelings for Emilio are real. It's not something I played up for the cameras," Sharleen said. "Emilio's not the bad-boy athlete the blogs make him out to be. He's sensitive and compassionate, and I love spending time with him."

Mrs. Fontaine's eyebrows rose and fell quickly. "I bet you do. One of his ex-lovers gave a tell-all interview with Channel 6 News this morning, and she said he's *very* well-endowed."

Too shocked to speak, she stared at her boss.

"I understand. Your hormones got the best of you, but don't do anything stupid like fall in love. It doesn't last." Mrs. Fontaine's voice carried a bitter edge, and a scowl twisted her lips. "Emilio's a superstar athlete who'll never be faithful to you."

Sharleen remained silent, stunned. Her body was

weary, desperate for sleep, and thinking about her troubled relationship only made her feel worse.

"You have what it takes to go far in this business, and I'd hate for you to throw it all away for a guy who'll never commit to you."

A headache pounded in her temples, and her throat closed up. Something Emilio had said weeks earlier, during one of their morning coaching sessions, came back to mind, and Sharleen smiled despite the overwhelming weight of her sadness.

"I never wanted a family for fear of losing them one day, but then I met you and now it's all I think about," he'd said, pulling her into his arms and brushing his lips softly against hers. *"You're the best thing that's ever happened to me."*

The memory brought her comfort, filled her with hope. Sharleen admired Mrs. Fontaine and thought she was a smart businesswoman, but she was wrong about Emilio. They were soul mates, not just sex buddies, and he'd never do anything to hurt her.

"I hope you have more ideas on how to attract new clients, because our LA clinic opens next month, and the more publicity the better."

"I became a life coach to help people transform their lives, not to become famous. If you can't respect that, I'll have no choice but to resign."

Mrs. Fontaine's eyes filled with fear, and the smile slid off her face. "Y-you don't mean that," she stammered, fussing with her scarf.

"Yes, I do. I can always freelance or start my own clinic right here in Atlanta…"

"You wouldn't!"

Sharleen cocked her head to the right. "Just watch me."

"I want us to be partners, not adversaries—"

"Then make me an offer I can't refuse."

The silence was deafening, and several seconds ticked off the wall clock.

"I'll increase your salary by ten percent *and* give you six weeks' paid vacation…" Mrs. Fontaine began.

"*And* you'll rehire Jocelyn," Sharleen said. "Jocelyn deserves her old job back, and that's one issue I won't concede on."

Mrs. Fontaine sat back in her chair, then slowly nodded her head. "It's a deal."

The women shook hands and shared a smile.

"To celebrate your promotion I've arranged a small soiree tonight at Dolce Vita at six o'clock," Mrs. Fontaine explained. "You're more than welcome to invite Emilio, and your family members as well."

Sharleen struggled with her words. She was thrilled about her promotion and wanted to celebrate with her friends and colleagues at her favorite restaurant, but she wanted to see Emilio before he left for Milan. *Should I go to my promotion party or Emilio's estate?* It was the biggest decision of Sharleen's life, and she didn't know what to do.

Chapter 19

"Are you sure you want to do this?"

Emilio scowled at his silver-haired pit-crew chief, wishing the loud Irishman would leave him alone. Lockland Walsh was working his last nerve, and he was sick of his questions. On Fridays the Atlanta Motor Speedway was filled with race-car fans of all ages desperate for a behind-the-scenes view of America's most dangerous and thrilling sport, and Emilio wanted to give the cheering spectators a good show. "I'm here, aren't I?"

"Kill the attitude. I'm not in the mood for your crap today." Lockland limped around the car, inspecting the tires, stress lines wrinkling his forehead. "Have you talked to your girl yet?"

"What does that have to do with me going for a spin around the track?"

"You're kidding, right? You've been off this week, and you know it. You clipped a visitor tour bus on Monday afternoon, and yesterday you drove over my foot."

Emilio dropped his gaze to the ground, so Lockland couldn't see the guilt in his eyes. He'd apologized and bought his pit-crew boss dinner to make amends, but he still felt horrible for hurting the grandfather of six. "It was an honest mistake," he mumbled, for lack of anything better to say. "It could happen to anybody."

"Get your head in the game," Lockland said, leveling a finger at him. "Focus."

Emilio nodded and tugged on his leather gloves. "I know what I'm doing. I got this."

"You better, or you'll end up in a body cast!"

The other guys in his pit crew snickered.

Hearing whistles and cheers, Emilio glanced over his shoulder. Hundreds of people were standing against the metal fence, waving signs bearing his name and image. If he weren't in such a funk, he would have signed autographs for the children. He'd tossed and turned all night, reliving his argument with Sharleen, unable to put his sister's accusations out of his mind.

"I don't have all day. Get in and get going." Lockland clapped him hard on the shoulder and steered him over to the track. "Three laps should suffice."

Emilio put on his helmet and slid inside his custom-made Ferrari. He was going to miss using it for practice, but now that he had a new and improved race car he didn't need it anymore. Thankfully, Antwan had found a buyer, and Emilio could pay off his tax bill and put the whole ugly incident with the IRS behind him.

"Take it nice and easy. The media hounds are out here again today, looking for a story, so don't do anything crazy," he warned, his gaze darting around the field. "Come back in one piece."

Lockland tapped the hood of the car, signaling the track was clear, and Emilio took off down the strip like a rocket. He switched gears, and as his speed climbed... ninety...one hundred...one hundred and twenty...his excitement grew. Adrenaline coursed through his veins, gave him a mind-blowing rush. He loved being behind the wheel of his race car, loved how invincible he felt whipping around the track at two hundred miles an hour. There was nothing quite like it, no greater high—

You mean, besides making love to Sharleen, right? You lose control every time she clamps her legs around your waist.

Distracted by the erotic image that popped into his mind, he lost control of the car. It jerked violently to the left and spun out onto the grass. He maneuvered it back onto the track and slowly increased his speed. He knew Lockland was going to give him hell for daydreaming, but he struggled to focus, to keep his head in the game. Every day, nonstop, he thought about Sharleen and nothing else.

That morning, while he was washing his motorcycle, Antwan had stormed into his garage. Their argument played in Emilio's mind as he completed his second lap around the track.

"Why did you give Sharleen a ten-thousand-dollar bonus?" Emilio had asked, crossing his arms.

"Because you're a handful, and I didn't want her to quit!"

He'd been annoyed, pissed off by his manager's joke, but it was what Antwan had said seconds later that made his blood boil.

"Sharleen's going on tour with Rashad J," he'd said. "She leaves for LA tonight at six o'clock."

"What? That's insane! She just started working with him last week."

"I know, but he's been acting a fool for months, and label execs at Urban Beats Records need someone tough like Sharleen to keep him in line during his eighteen-city tour…"

Emilio gripped the steering wheel, imagined it was Rashad J's neck. Taking a deep breath didn't stop his mind from racing out of control. Was he overthinking things? Assuming the worst because ex-friends, lovers and relatives had betrayed his trust and used him to gain wealth and popularity? Emilio wasn't taking any chances. Not where Sharleen was concerned. He'd made a mistake walking out on her on Monday and had to apologize immediately. Punching the gas pedal with his foot, he felt the car zoom around the corner and fly down the track. *One more lap, then I'm out of here!* He had to see Sharleen before she left town. It was stressful, nerve-racking to think she was off somewhere with Rashad J.

Emilio banished the thought from his mind, refused to entertain it. He didn't want the Bedroom Maestro putting the moves on his girlfriend and realized, in that moment, how foolish he'd been. Sharleen hadn't forced him to come out of retirement—he'd made the decision alone. His love of the sport had been the driving factor, not anything she'd ever said or did during their coaching sessions.

Memories of better days, of all the times they'd talked and laughed, warmed his heart. Emilio pictured Sharleen now, in his mind's eye, and smiled for the first time in days. He'd never met anyone more loving and sincere and knew in his heart that she was the woman he was destined to spend his life with. Emilio wanted her back in his arms, where she belonged. But to get back in her good graces he'd have to humble himself...

As Emilio approached the finish line, he spotted a curvy female silhouette in a bold, mustard-yellow dress. He was seeing things, had to be, because the woman standing beside Lockland looked like Sharleen. His pulse pounded in his ear, and his heart soared to the sky. Emilio leaned forward in his seat, peered through the windshield, tried to focus his gaze. *It really* was *Sharleen!*

His chest puffed up with pride, as if he'd just won another championship, and a grin curled his lips. Seeing Sharleen made him more determined than ever to win her back. Her red lips held a pretty smile, her loose curls flapped in the breeze, and her figure-hugging dress was eye-catching. Emilio couldn't stop staring at her. His gaze slid over her chest, her hips, and down her silky brown legs. He licked his lips, remembered how incredible it felt being inside her and suddenly lost control of the wheel for the second time.

Emilio slammed on the brakes, stopping safely just in time. He jumped out of the car. He took off his helmet and gloves and tossed them to the ground. His pit crew ran over, wearing bewildered looks, but he ignored them. Sharleen had come to see him, and nothing else mattered.

She strode confidently toward him...twenty feet... ten feet...five feet... Emilio told himself not to rush her, to play it cool. But when she was close, he seized her around the waist and swept her into his arms. He inhaled her perfume, allowed the sweet, floral scent to wash over him. He couldn't keep his hands off of her, stroked her neck, shoulders and hips. Emilio didn't know how long he stood there, holding Sharleen, but when she pulled away he felt a profound sense of disappointment.

"I'm glad you're here," he said, with a broad smile. "I missed you."

"I didn't want you to leave for Milan until we cleared the air—"

"What makes you think I'm going to Milan?"

"Aren't you? Antwan told me you're leaving tonight for the Classic Car Show."

He returned her puzzled look. "Wait…aren't you going on tour with Rashad J?"

"No way!" she said, adamantly shaking her head. "The record label asked, but I refused. Why?"

Emilio hung his head. "Damn, I can't believe it. Antwan punked us again."

"That snake!" Sharleen said. "Let's go kick some butt at Elite Management."

"Slow down, Foxy Cleopatra!" he joked, affectionately patting her on the hips. "We can't kill Antwan. He brought us back together."

"You're right, but I still want to egg his office!"

He laughed. "God, I missed you," he said, nuzzling his chin against her cheek.

"Then why didn't you return any of my calls and texts?"

Emilio spotted a lanky photographer scaling the fence and tightened his hold around her waist. "Let's go to my private suite. We can talk there."

They walked through the pedestrian tunnel, past the gift shop and into the suite. It had theater-style seats, a fully stocked bar and flat-screen TVs. It offered panoramic views of the track and everything a fan could want while watching the big race. Emilio sat in his favorite chair and pulled Sharleen down on his lap. He loved feeling her warmth, stroking her skin and playing in her lush, thick hair.

"How did you know I was here?" he asked. "I didn't even know I was coming to practice until I pulled into the parking lot!"

"Francesca told me where to find you."

His eyes widened. *My sister did* what?

"I went to your estate, and Francesca invited me inside. I told her the truth about the bonus, my friendship with Antwan and my professional background. I wanted her to know I'm not after your money, and that I have a career I'm proud of."

"I appreciate that, Sharleen. I had a long talk with Francesca this morning during breakfast, and she admitted that she's jealous of you—"

"That's crazy! Why?"

"Because you're everything she's not. Ambitious, successful and financially independent." To make her laugh, Emilio cocked an eyebrow and wiggled his nose. "*And* you have a rich, handsome boyfriend, too."

"Yeah, a rich, handsome boyfriend who walked out on me four days ago."

He heard the pain in her voice, the sadness, and felt like a jerk for hurting her feelings. Her words tore him up inside, made him feel guilty for losing his cool that day. "I'm sorry," he said, tenderly stroking her hands. "I was angry, and I knew if I didn't walk away I'd end up saying something I'd regret."

"I thought we had something special, Emilio. I thought you loved me—"

"I do," he insisted, desperate to get through to her. "One argument won't change the way I feel about you, Sharleen. I adore you, and that will never change."

"How could you think I'd betray you? That I'd ever do anything to hurt you?"

Emilio coughed to clear the lump in his throat. He wasn't raised to share his feelings, and had long buried the pain of his past, but he wanted Sharleen to know the truth. "Before I was a race-car driver, nobody wanted anything to do with me. I was a shy, overweight teenager. But once I won my first championship, I couldn't keep the girls off me."

Sharleen leaned into him and nodded.

"I've had my fair share of one-night stands, but I've never had a serious relationship."

"Never?"

"Never," he said quietly, shaking his head. "Francesca's always looked out for me, so when she told me about the bonus and showed me the pictures online I assumed the worst. I felt stupid, as if you'd tricked me. I thought the only reason you slept with me was to advance your career."

"Emilio, I'm not that kind of girl. I don't care about fame. I only care about you."

"I know, and deep down in my heart I knew I was wrong. But it wasn't until I spoke to Antwan that I realized how stupid I'd been."

"What are we going to do about Francesca? I still don't think she likes me."

"Leave her to me. She'll come around."

"And if she doesn't?"

"Then I'll buy her something expensive from Louis Vuitton, write your name on the card and have it delivered to her apartment. Trust me, she'll be your new BFF!"

Sharleen laughed and playfully swatted his shoulder. "Emilio, stop it. I'm serious."

"So am I. You mean everything to me, and I won't let anyone tear us apart."

"I got the VP position," she said, a shy smile on her glossy red lips. "I officially start on Monday."

"Congratulations, baby. You deserve it, and I'm proud of you."

A look of pure joy covered her face. "You are? You really mean that?"

"Of course I am." He met her gaze, lovingly stared into her eyes. "Your career is important to you, so it's important to me. But there's no way in hell I'm letting you travel alone with Rashad J or any of your other male clients. That stops now, understood?"

The sound of her effervescent laugh made Emilio feel ten feet high, as if he'd finally done something right. "How did I get so lucky?" he said aloud, giving her a peck on the cheek.

"Luck had nothing to do with it. Antwan tricked us!" Sharleen linked her arms around his neck. "Emilio, I love you with all my heart, and I always will."

"And I love you. Thank you for making me a better man and for not giving up on me. I haven't felt this good in years, and you're the reason why."

"What now?" she asked, snuggling against him. "Where do we go from here?"

"Back to my estate to make love for the third, fourth and fifth time…" he whispered, brushing his lips against her earlobe. "You're the best part of me, and I can't live another day without you. I want to go to bed every night and wake up every morning with you in my arms."

"That could be arranged." Sharleen tilted her head to the side and batted her eyelashes at him. "*Mrs. Emilio Morretti* has a nice ring to it, don't you think?"

"It sounds like music to my ears."

"Good. Now shut up and kiss me!"

Emilio tossed his head back and laughed freely. "All right, Madam Vice President. One slow, sensuous kiss coming right up."

He cupped her chin and lowered his mouth to hers to seal the deal. Consumed by love, he kissed her with a ferocious passion, with all the desire and hunger coursing through his veins. He buried his hands in her hair, pulled her closer to deepen the kiss. Emilio had finally found the woman of his dreams, his Mrs. Right, and he was going to cherish her every day for the rest of their lives.

* * * * *

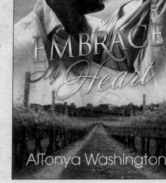

They have
an undeniable
attraction....

SNOWY
MOUNTAIN
NIGHTS

LINDSAY
EVANS

The last person Reyna Allen expects to run into while vacationing is
Garrison Richards, her ex-husband's divorce lawyer. Garrison is good
at his job—a little too good—but he wants to show Reyna that he has
since found his moral compass. But as their mutual heat thaws her
resolve, will doubts put the freeze on their relationship before he can
convince her that they're meant for happily-ever-after?

**"The author has exceptional skills in painting the scenery, making it
easy for readers to visualize the story as it unfolds."
—*RT Book Reviews* on *PLEASURE UNDER THE SUN***

Available March 2015!

HARLEQUIN®
™ www.Harlequin.com

KPLE3950315

REQUEST YOUR FREE BOOKS!

2 FREE NOVELS
PLUS 2 FREE GIFTS!

KIMANI™
ROMANCE

Love's ultimate destination!

KROM13R

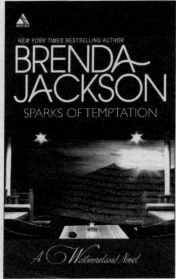

KPBJI700215R

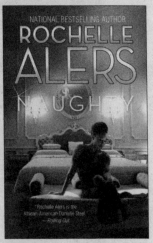